Born and raised on the Wirral Peninsula in England, **Charlotte Hawkes** is mum to two intrepid boys who love her to play building block games with them, and who object loudly to the amount of time she spends on the computer. When she isn't writing—or building with blocks—she is company director for a small Anglo/French construction firm. Charlotte loves to hear from readers, and you can contact her at her website: charlotte-hawkes.com.

Also by Charlotte Hawkes

Falling for the Single Dad Surgeon

Reunited on the Front Line miniseries

Second Chance with His Army Doc
Reawakened by Her Army Major

Royal Christmas at Seattle General collection

Falling for the Secret Prince
by Alison Roberts
Neurosurgeon's Christmas to Remember
by Traci Douglass
The Bodyguard's Christmas Proposal
The Princess's Christmas Baby
by Louisa George

Available now

Discover more at millsandboon.co.uk.

THE DOCTOR'S ONE NIGHT TO REMEMBER

CHARLOTTE HAWKES

MILLS & BOON

First published in Great Britain 2021
by Mills & Boon, an imprint of HarperCollins*Publishers* Ltd,
1 London Bridge Street, London, SE1 9GF

www.harpercollins.co.uk

HarperCollins*Publishers*
1st Floor, Watermarque Building,
Ringsend Road, Dublin 4, Ireland

Large Print edition 2021

The Doctor's One Night to Remember © 2021 Charlotte Hawkes

ISBN: 978-0-263-28789-9

07/21

To Helen.
For the walks, the giggles, and the
odd jogs…though our boat experiences
were never quite like Isla's! xx

CHAPTER ONE

'WHICH ONE OF them is faking it, do you think?' Isla Sinclair wondered breezily, as she eyed the honeymooning couple frolicking together on the Chilean beach.

Her stepsister Leonora—former stepsister, if Isla was going to be strictly accurate—put down her summer cocktail and turned gracefully to look.

'Don't let what Brad-the-Cad did turn you into some hardened cynic, Isla.' Leo smiled softly. 'Maybe they're actually in love?'

'And you're such a hopeless romantic.' Isla grinned, making a conscious effort to thrust any unwelcome memories of her ex-fiancé out of her head. 'You know as well as I do that someone is always faking it. If they're really lucky, then they're enjoying a mutually advantageous marriage, like my mother and your father had.'

Or at least it had been mutually advantageous for a blissful five years, ending perfectly amicably thirteen years ago, when Isla and Leo had been nineteen.

Onwards and upwards. Certainly that was a lesson Isla had learned at the knee of her beautiful, charming mother who had bounced her, cooed to her and whispered to her just what had to be done in order to negotiate for her next, richer, even more well-connected husband.

Marianna Sinclair-Raleigh-Burton had always seen marriage more like a business negotiation, with each party agreeing in advance what the other would bring to the table.

'I can just hear your mother now.' Leo shook her head affectionately. *'Why complicate things by pretending to be in love, girls? Far better to be up-front. That way, there are no nasty surprises.'*

'Ugh!' Isla mimicked one of her mother's comical, yet simultaneously elegant shudders. 'Perish the thought.'

Leo laughed, a tinkly kind of sound that Isla had always thought was the prettiest laugh she'd ever heard.

'You sound just like her, Isla.'

'I can live with that. Where is my mother anyway?'

'She said she was going to have a lie-down.'

Leo pulled a wry face. 'But what are the chances she's found herself a new suitor?'

'Well, firstly, she's a new divorcee, *again.*' Isla ticked the points off on her fingers. 'Secondly, she insisted on coming out here and turning it into a holiday, even though I told her that I had come out early for some quiet, to get my head around my new role as ship's doctor in two days. And thirdly, she booked us into the most expensive hotel in this part of the region—possibly in the whole of Chile. So if she hasn't already eyed up a new husband for herself then I'd be surprised.'

'Better her looking for herself than trying to set one of us two up,' Leo groaned, though there was no rancour in her tone.

Both girls knew that, for all her faults, Marianna was the closest thing Leo had ever had to a mother, even all these years after their respective parents' divorce. And in Isla's eyes too, Marianna was the most loving, generous mother she thought a girl could ever have.

Still, that didn't stop her from rolling her eyes good-naturedly now. 'Quite. But I won't hold my breath.'

'Me neither.' Leo turned to eye the honeymoon couple again. 'Maybe they really are in love.'

'Maybe.'

With a sigh, Isla let her eyes drift back to them. They certainly looked like they were loving life.

It just wasn't the life that Isla had ever wanted for herself.

'Anyway, I fancy checking out a few little stores I saw on the walk down here.' Leo finished her drink and pushed it to the side. 'Do you want to come?'

Isla hesitated for a moment. 'No, actually, if you don't mind I think I'd like to go for a walk along the beach. Once I'm on board, it might be a while before I get a chance to set foot on land again.'

'Makes sense.' Leo slipped off the stool and hooked her summery purse over her head. 'See you back at the hotel?'

'Yeah, about an hour?'

'An hour.' Leo nodded, heading daintily out of the bar and, unsurprisingly, in the direction of the honeymooners.

Typically romantic Leo. Isla smiled to herself.

But she definitely wasn't here for love, or even for a holiday romance—the idea of either was enough to make her shudder—she was here for work. Better than that, she was here for the job of her life, the job she'd dreamed of doing ever since she'd been a kid—junior doctor on a cruise ship.

The *Jewel of Hestia.*

Perhaps not the incredible *Queen Cassiopeia*, the flagship of the Port-Star Cruise Line fleet that was anchored out at sea right now, but a good one all the same. One that would allow her to do the work she loved combined with travelling around the world.

What could be more perfect?

And if it also got her away from the humiliation of Bradley, and away from her mother's next shenanigans, then wasn't that a bonus?

Downing the last of her drink, Isla stood up and made herself smile. This wasn't about the past; this was about the future. Or, until her ship sailed into port in a couple of days' time, this was about living in the present and exploring as much as she could of what this part of Chile had to offer.

The sudden commotion behind her made Isla spin around to where an argument between two young men was going on in the next bar. Two six-foot, muscle-bound lads squaring—rather drunkenly—up to each other, both of whom might have looked at home in a boxing ring.

Clearly, the crowd seemed to think so. As much as they were entertained, they were evidently keeping their distance, not wanting to get caught in the middle.

That's my cue.

Weaving through the tables, the occupants of which were mostly focused on the fact that the argument was turning into a brawl, Isla made her way to the strip of walkway between the bars and the beach and turned in the opposite direction from the fight. And the loud crash that ensued.

It wasn't her business, and she didn't care. She kept her head down and picked up her pace, right up to the moment when a deafening crash split the air.

Isla's heart jolted and she whirled around despite herself—just in time to see a ship's officer vaulting over the barrier to the sand and racing to haul one of the drunken young men—still flailing and punching—off the one who was now lying unconscious on the ground, as though the lad weighed little more than a sack of potatoes.

With one word, the newcomer had the crowd flipping from ghoulish spectators to concerned citizens, grouping around the injured party and checking him over, whilst the officer pinned the still-agitated second lad to a concrete pillar to stop him from reaching his quarry to rain down yet more punches.

The officer was at least as tall as the would-be boxer and, even though he wasn't as obviously bulked up, there was no doubt that he was strong and skilled enough to control the bigger man, apparently quietly and smoothly talking him down before pressing a couple of the other stronger locals into taking the lad further away until he calmed down completely. Then he pulled a walkie-talkie from his waist and issued more instructions into that.

It was mesmerising how smoothly and efficiently the man had seemed to take charge of a situation which could have escalated far too easily. Her heart jolted again, and she told herself it was nothing more than an adrenalin rush due to the situation. Or perhaps it was because it highlighted, so aptly, all of her ex's failings. Brad had liked to pretend that he was that kind of bark-a-command-and-everyone-jumps alpha male, but the truth was that he'd been more of a make-the-bullets-for-someone-else-to-fire kind of a man.

So what did it say about her that it had taken her so long to see the truth?

Enough! Isla chastised silently, shaking the guilt and shame from her thoughts. This was why she was here in Chile, waiting for the *Jewel of Hestia* to arrive. The ship's junior doctor wasn't just a new career; it was to be a new start.

Isla turned to leave, when suddenly she heard a

series of shouts, mostly for emergency services, and then one shout which she couldn't ignore.

'*Médico? Es alguien médico?*'

Swinging back, her stomach lurching slightly, she surveyed the severity of the scene for a moment. Almost hoping someone else might step forward.

Nobody did.

'*Soy médica,*' she muttered at length, stumbled forward and pushed her way through the tight throng, her eyes taking in each detail as it came into focus.

Close up, she could now see that the man who had fallen had crashed through a glass-laden table and was now lying on his back on the ground, the table and shards of glass beneath him. Blood pooled somewhere around his lower back.

'You.' Isla pointed to some random gawking bystanders as she quickly and efficiently picked her way through the debris. 'Can you move the tables? *Mover las mesas?*'

She crouched down beside the casualty, but until the glass was swept away she didn't dare kneel.

'And you…a sweeping brush…*un cepillo para…*' her brain scrabbled for the words '…*para barrer los…fragmentos de vidrio.*'

She only paused long enough to see the bartender acknowledge her before she turned her focus to the patient. Not unconscious after all, but certainly groggy.

'Hello, can you tell me your name? *Cómo se llama?*'

He groaned and weakly tried to push her hand away, possibly hearing her but not processing her words. Another observation to file away for the ambulance crew.

'Okay—you're okay. I'm a doctor. *Soy médica.*'

A quick check of his pulse suggested an erratic beat, hardly surprising after a bar fight and then demolishing a glass table. But there were no shards on his front, which meant the blood had to be coming from an injury on his back.

'Someone has called for an ambulance? *Ambulancia?*'

'*Sí, sí,*' several people relayed at once, flowing into a torrent of Chilean Spanish that Isla wasn't entirely sure she understood.

At least the barman had now swept away the worst of the broken glass and she could tend to the patient, although the guy was big and muscular and moving him was proving harder than she'd expected.

'Help me roll him onto his front,' she instructed anyone who was listening. '*Ayudar me...rodar...*'

'Leave him, please.'

Isla jerked her head up at the commanding voice, unprepared for the man who was bearing down on her. The cruise ship officer from before—as if her body hadn't already prickled in awareness. She told herself it was just the heat—the downdraught that his body created as he moved closer—and nothing more.

Her eyes seemed intent on drinking in every inch of him, not least the epaulettes on his shoulders. A senior officer, at that. A first officer—practically the Captain's right-hand man.

'I take it he's one of yours?' she bit out, furious with herself. 'Good—you can tell me his name?'

'He is one of mine,' First Officer McHotty growled. 'And he clearly needs a doctor.'

'I *am* a doctor.'

'Is that so?' He barely paused a fraction of a beat. 'What I mean is that we have our own doctors to deal with our crew.'

'Right, but they aren't here, are they?' Isla kept her eyes on the patient, her hands finding a good purchase. 'However, I *am* here, and he's bleeding out. So I suggest you help me roll him. And tell me his name. Oh, and what language does he speak?'

She sensed rather than saw the moment of hesitation as McHotty took in the scene for himself, but she was having enough trouble focusing.

Impressive enough from a distance, up close he was also possibly the most breathtaking specimen of a male that Isla thought she'd ever seen, as galling as that was to admit. He wasn't classically handsome; that would have been too banal for the man. Instead there was an arresting quality about him, from the sharp, square jaw to the blade of a nose. His eyes were the richest, deepest caramel she'd ever seen, with a smokiness to match that raw masculine voice. And his body? Her brain refused to go there—she didn't even want to start *thinking* about his body.

It was unfortunate then that her brain didn't appear to be in control of anything right now. Despite all her silent cerebral protestations, her eyes slid—seemingly of their own volition—to the body crouched down beside her.

The powerful thighs brushing hers, and unwittingly sending little bolts of electricity through her. His pristine uniform clung like a lover to hewn muscle, from strong thighs, to contoured torso, to wide shoulders—no wonder he'd had little trouble besting the brawny would-be fighter.

If the world had stopped spinning, Isla wouldn't have been all that surprised, and yet the entire interaction took less than a couple of seconds.

Nonetheless, it galled her beyond all measure that her mouth felt parched as her eyes drank it all in. As if she'd never seen a man before in her life.

Only, if she were to be honest, she'd certainly never seen a man like *this* before. Surely the hottest male specimen to have ever walked the planet? And, judging by the doe-eyed females in the crowd, she definitely wasn't the only one to think it.

Isla thrust the traitorous thought aside and forced her attention back to her unexpected patient.

'What language, please?' she repeated, as firmly as she could.

'His name is Philippe. He can speak English.'

'Okay, Philippe, I'm Isla, I'm a doctor, I'm here to help you. We're going to roll you onto your stomach, okay?' she warned, as McHotty crouched down beside her—so close that it made her feel altogether too many sensations in too many places, the heat seeping from his body into hers playing havoc with her insides.

Then he took the patient, rolling the muscle-bound hulk as if he weighed nothing.

The crowd collectively sucked in a breath.

A long, sharp shard of glass was protruding from the man's left buttock, blood surrounding the area. There was no doubt that it had severed his superior gluteal artery.

As her new, unwelcome companion grabbed his walkie and issued another irate command for the ship's doctor, Isla looked around for some material, eventually settling on her own chiffony scarf. Wrapping it around her hand, she prepared to grab the shard.

'What are you doing now?' McHotty demanded abruptly, dropping back next to her.

'I need to remove the glass.'

'If you remove it, won't he just bleed all the more? Or can you tourniquet it?'

'I can't tourniquet his backside.' She shook her head, drawing the shard out carefully. 'And yes, the artery will need occluding.'

'I suggest you would do better to leave it in place,' he continued in a voice which bore little resemblance to a suggestion and entirely too much like a command. 'Certainly until my ship's doctor arrives.'

This last comment was clearly a slight. She'd heard them before; there was no reason this should rankle more just because it was coming from this stranger.

She forced herself to keep her tone even. 'Your ship's doctor is taking their time. Time this patient may not have.'

She could tell that he was caught between wanting to make another call and not leaving her alone with his crewman. What did it say about her that she got a tiny kick out of unsettling this man, who was clearly acutely accustomed to being the one in control?

'Not when he's unconscious and his heartbeat is so erratic. What if he suddenly needs CPR? Also, it's best to remove glass immediately to reduce the risk of infection, and to prevent any allergic response. I need to remove the foreign body and clean the wound.'

'Not just a patient. *My* crewman. You will wait.'

'I'm afraid not. You might be second in command on that floating city out at sea, but right here, right now, this is a medical emergency and *I'm* the only doctor on scene. So you need to wind your neck in; we're doing it my way.'

Had she really just told a man who was senior enough to be her boss to *wind his neck in?*

When was the last time anyone had got under her skin the way that he seemed to have done?

She could practically feel the castigation in his glower; it *zinged* through her.

'You misunderstand...' he growled, and a lesser woman might have quaked at the warning tone in his voice.

After Bradley, Isla had certainly had enough of being the *lesser woman*.

'There,' she cut in, holding aloft the long shard and smiling sweetly. 'All out.'

The giant of a man glanced down, and she could swear, just for a fraction of a moment, that he blanched. So fleeting that she thought she might have imagined it.

'He's still bleeding,' McHotty rasped. 'How are you going to stop that now?'

'Like this,' she said grimly, quickly cleaning up the wound and plugging it with her finger.

As though it was every day that she stared at the hottest man she'd ever seen in her life whilst her finger was plugging some other guy's arse cheek. Worse, she was almost sure she saw amusement flicker over his impossibly arresting features.

'See?' She glowered. 'Now where's that damned ambulance?'

Nikhil Dara listened as the doctor—*Isla*, she'd said her name was—wound up her handover to the emergency services, and instructed himself to concentrate on how efficiently she performed her job, rather than how particularly ravishing she was. It was surprisingly difficult—certainly for him.

He knew his reputation for being single-minded, and exacting—as well as several less polite terms his crew used, particularly when they were exhausted and he was making them run a scenario one more time to ensure that it was *right*. Rather than balk at such nicknames, however, he had always prided himself on them. Yet now, for the first time in memory, he found himself struggling to focus purely on the task in hand without letting his gaze slide to the arresting doctor.

As if being at sea meant he'd somehow been deprived of female company when the truth was that his life as First Officer on a cruise liner often entailed women—crew and passengers—offering themselves up to him daily on a silver platter. On one occasion, quite literally.

He never bit.

Certainly never on board and, if on shore, then never with anyone he would see again. It was a measure of control on which he prided himself. Which made it all the more aggravating that he seemed to have to fight his own body to keep his distance from the young doctor, as he concentrated on instructing his recently arrived junior officer to accompany Philippe in the ambulance and then for said officer to keep him informed of the hospital's progress.

Helping the crew to close the doors, he watched the vehicle speed off and finally turned to the doctor and bobbed his head in acknowledgement.

'Thank you for your help. Philippe is fortunate that you were there.'

'No problem.' She shrugged, hauling out her phone for a moment and frowning as she read some message.

There was no reason on earth for him to wonder what it was that had irritated her. Or why he should notice quite how her blue eyes looked almost silvery-grey when she nodded back and swung away from him. Or how her golden-brown hair skimmed her shoulders from the ponytail high on the back of her head.

Ridiculously fanciful, he berated himself, with a rough shake of his head. As if he could dislodge the ball of pressure that had been squatting on his brain for days, pressing up against his skull, creating a dull throb. One that no amount of headache medication could hope to touch.

He wasn't himself.

He hadn't been since he'd received the birthday card from Daksh yesterday.

Daksh. The brother he hadn't heard from in over two decades but who now, out of the blue, apparently wanted to meet. Right here, in Chile.

How the hell Daksh had even tracked him

down was beyond him. But, worse than that, the man who was his brother in nothing but name was stirring up old ghosts that should be left buried. Preferably as deep as possible.

Better yet, left to burn in some hell at the centre of the earth.

Nikhil cursed silently. No wonder his head was all over the place. No wonder he was letting the attraction for this woman, this stranger, get under his skin. If he'd been himself, he would have dismissed it as simple physical attraction—pleasant enough but best left unexplored in the middle of a cruise.

He tried to clear his head.

'Okay,' offered the young doctor when the silence stretched out an uncomfortable touch too long. 'Well, I guess I should be going.'

Without warning, something twisted and darted within Nikhil's veins. The sudden realisation that a few more steps and she would be gone. Inexplicably, he found that he didn't want her to leave.

'Wait.' The command was out before he even realised he was going to issue it.

She stopped, then turned back slowly. As if she didn't really want to, but felt compelled.

As compelled as he did? The notion was fascinating.

'Let me buy you a drink.'

She stared at him, not blinking.

'No,' she managed at last, and he had the oddest notion that it was harder for her than she thought it should have been.

'Why not?' He grinned, liking the way her eyes darted to his mouth, and then she flushed.

As if her thoughts weren't entirely proper.

'Because I don't even know your name,' she blurted out, and then squeezed her eyes shut, suggesting that she hadn't intended to say that.

'Nikhil.' He inclined his head. 'And you're Isla.'

She looked surprised, and Nikhil shrugged. 'You told Philippe your name, even though he was unconscious.'

'Right.' She bobbed her head. 'Well, you can never be sure how much a person can hear, even then.'

'So I've heard,' he acknowledged.

It was a topic that had long interested him, yet right now he couldn't think of anything less fascinating.

'Now introductions have been made, how about that drink?'

'I…' She pulled a rueful face, tailing off into a telling silence.

'As a thank you.'

Why was he pushing this? He should just return to the ship, finish up his shift and get ready for his rare evening onshore. Alone. Instead, he heard himself speaking again.

'The company will want to take your details—for their report. I can guide you through filling it out.'

It was true, but it hadn't been the thought at the forefront of his mind. Odd, since it ought to have been.

'It's okay. I can provide a report of my own if necessary.'

There was something in his tone that he couldn't quite place. He found that he didn't care for the way it unbalanced him. He'd spent years ensuring nothing, and no one, ever rattled him. Yet this woman affected him like no one else ever had.

It had to be that damned birthday card he'd received yesterday from his brother. If 'brother' was what you could call the stranger Nikhil hadn't heard anything from in practically two decades.

'The forms are unnecessarily convoluted,' he warned, shutting down the other, errant thought.

'I just had my finger in your crewman's arse cheek. A ship's form doesn't faze me.'

A ghost of a smile played at her mouth, and it

seemed to jolt through his entire body. Somehow, it was more than just attraction. He was well-versed in sexual chemistry, and equally skilled at controlling it, not giving in to it. But this was… different. She—*Isla*—got to him. And he didn't care for such a realisation.

'Is that so?'

'It is.' She bobbed her head. 'I may not be one of the doctors on *your* ship, but I am actually Port-Star Cruise's newest doctor.'

'Say again?'

She laughed unexpectedly and her face lit up so stunningly, so vibrantly, that for a moment he was sure she'd eclipsed the hot Chilean sun.

Suddenly he realised he wanted more of that smile. More of that joy. As if he'd taken a shot of something earth-shaking. And now he needed more.

'You work for Port-Star?'

'I do. The *Jewel of Hestia* will come into this port in two days' time, and it will be my first assignment.'

'A new career move then?' he mused. 'All the more reason to celebrate, surely.'

And although it should have been a question, Nikhil realised that it hadn't been.

'Dinner, I think. I'll collect you around seven-thirty. Where are you staying?'

'What if I have a boyfriend?' she asked, but he could tell it was more curiosity than refusal.

'You don't,' he answered simply. 'You have a line where you have recently removed a ring. Judging by the width of it, I'd say an engagement ring, not a wedding ring. And, as you just said, your assignment on the *Hestia* will be your first. So, a fresh start.'

And if the fact that he'd noticed so much about her in so short a time worried him, he was determined to ignore it.

She stared at him for a long moment, those expressive eyes of hers threatening to draw him in with every sweep of her gaze.

What the hell was he doing?

'Fine,' she answered after what seemed like for ever. 'I don't have a boyfriend, but I have… friends here, with me. I can't just ditch them.'

'You've ditched them now,' he pointed out. 'Or they've ditched you. Either way, you clearly don't live in each other's pockets. You have your last night with them tomorrow, and presumably that's the big farewell meal, so you're free to meet me tonight.'

She opened her mouth but then closed it again.

She was tempted…and that gave him more of a kick than it had any right to.

'Plus it's my birthday—are you really going to leave me to celebrate it alone?'

Why the hell had he told her that?

Fury shot through him. It had to be Daksh's letter and imperious command to meet that had rattled him.

He never told anyone when his birthday was.

If he were honest, Nikhil didn't know why it was such a secret, or how it had come to be this big thing. Nor did he know quite why he got such a kick out of the fact that no one on board knew. Perhaps it was because, in these close-quarter confines, everybody knew everything about everyone else's business and this was one little nugget he could keep to himself—save for the Captain and HR, both of whom would have been in breach for divulging it.

Yet now he'd just announced it to the newest member of Port-Star. It should have been his cue to turn around and walk. Instead, he heard himself speaking again.

'Which hotel then, Isla?'

Her blue-grey eyes sparked, and yet still she didn't shut him down.

'Okay,' she answered suddenly, biting out the name quickly.

His eyebrows shot up; too late, he wished he hadn't reacted. But that hotel was well-known to be a playground for the rich and famous. Certainly not somewhere the average ship's officer might stay, not even a doctor, and the last thing he wanted to do was get involved with the monied crowd.

They, apparently, were more his brother's crowd than his.

'A farewell gift from my…friends,' Isla said suddenly, as if reading his thoughts. Though he could tell she was holding something back. 'We thought we'd push the boat out, if you'll pardon the pun.'

He could understand that. Didn't he do the same thing each year, when he booked twelve months ahead just to eat in Chile's world-renowned Te Tinca restaurant?

Alone.

'Ah. And they can't spare you for an evening?'

So why was he now insisting on the stunning doctor accompanying him?

It had to be his way of avoiding Daksh.

'I… They… I suppose they could,' she hazarded after a moment. 'Not a date, of course.'

'Of course not,' he demurred. 'Well, Little Doc, shall we say seven-thirty? In this lobby.'

And then, before anything else could be said— or any more damage done—Nikhil turned around and strode away.

CHAPTER TWO

ISLA DIDN'T KNOW what had possessed her to agree to dinner with Nikhil.

Or at least that was what she tried to tell herself.

She could pretend that it was because of the text she'd received from her mother moments before Nikhil had asked her for that drink. Even as she'd been walking away from him, she'd seen the message demanding to know where she was. More than that, she'd been able to practically hear her mother's excitement in every word, as Marianna had crowed about finding the most perfect new man for her to meet.

Isla shuddered, just as she had back then. The last thing she wanted was a blind date, or any date, really. Which was why her head had been calmly telling her to politely decline Nikhil's offer, even whilst her skin had been on fire and her insides had been jostling as if her organs were playing a game of musical chairs.

But then, instead of a refusal, she'd listened

to that devilish voice in her head telling her that the best way to avoid being pressed into a blind date by her mother would be to tell her that she already had a date—with a First Officer, no less.

It was a logical solution. But, deep down, Isla suspected that her motives weren't quite so logical. If she was honest, she might suspect that they had less to do with practicality and more to do with the way that Nikhil had made her body feel...alive.

Just by looking at her. There had been more chemistry between her and this relative stranger than she thought she'd ever felt with Brad.

And wasn't that rather sad?

Certainly it explained why she was now standing in front of the mirror, trying to quash some unwanted thrill as she critically assessed her sixth outfit choice so far, like the kind of teenager she had never really been.

She might have spoken to Leo, but her former stepsister didn't seem to have got back to the hotel either. Isla tried not to take that as *fate* giving her a naughty little push.

Staring at her outfit again, she heaved a sigh. She *never* dithered over her clothing choices. And her room had certainly never looked as though she'd emptied the contents of the closet onto her bed. That was for other girls. Just as the rich lipstick was, purchased barely two hours ago from the hotel's extortionately priced boutique.

Ridiculous.

There was taking the opportunity to avoid a blind date set up by her mother, and then there was dressing up as though this dinner with Nikhil was a date in itself.

Well, it wasn't happening.

Marching into the bathroom, she wiped the lipstick off her mouth and threw the tube into the bin and marched back out into the bedroom. Then she proceeded to quickly and neatly put all the clothes back onto the hangers and away, as though she could restore some order into her suddenly uncharacteristically topsy-turvy world.

And if her hands were shaking slightly, and her eyes kept flying to the clock to see that the digits had barely changed from the last time she'd checked, then at least no one else but her would ever know.

Finally, her room was clear again. Pristine. Ordered. The way she liked it. Isla checked the clock again. Five minutes had passed.

This was ridiculous.

She was acting like an adolescent, wound up for her first date. The worst of it was that she'd never acted this way even when she *had* been an adolescent. Snatching up her purse and sliding her room key card inside, Isla stepped out of her room and strode down the hall to the elevators.

He was just a man, like any other, she reminded herself as she jabbed irritably at the buttons. And if her traitorous brain was having trouble remembering that simple fact, then a walk around the town for half an hour should be enough to clear her head and get things in order.

The elevator bounced slightly as it stopped at the ground floor, the doors opening with an efficient *swish* as the sounds of an Argentine tango, and plenty of chatter, filled her ears.

The distraction was so much better than the quiet of her room. She even felt empowered by the way her heels clicked on the marble floor.

This was just a *thank you* dinner, from the First Officer of the ship whose crewman she'd just helped. Nothing more.

Then she lifted her eyes, only for them to slam into Nikhil's as he sat in the lobby, barely fifteen metres away, his powerful frame making the large wingback look almost fragile as he lounged. One ankle was balanced casually on the knee of his other leg, a large broadsheet in his hands, yet he looked even more arcane and forbidding than he had a few hours earlier. Her entire body seemed to turn to liquid. Boiling hot liquid that bubbled through her veins and smouldered in her chest, leaving her almost feverish.

And that was before he unfolded his legs with a casualness she didn't know why she thought was deceptive, and stood up. Her breath caught in a hard ball in her chest.

His body—which had looked hewn enough in his officer's uniform—somehow appeared even more dangerous clad in his own clothes. Even more lethal. She thought she might even have swayed slightly, feeling momentarily light-headed, as if she'd had several drinks too many, when the truth was that she hadn't touched a drop.

It isn't a real date, she said desperately to herself. *It's just dinner, and it's just to avoid Marianna's latest blind date set-up.*

Isla wasn't sure her brain was listening. The guy was positively intoxicating and now she'd started drinking him in she seemed wholly incapable of dragging her gaze away. Even as he approached, it was all Isla could do not to lift her hands, though to ward him off or pull him closer she was afraid she couldn't be certain.

'You're early,' she managed instead, barely recognising the husky quality of her voice.

'As are you,' Nikhil countered dryly. 'It's a welcome surprise.'

Any other time she might have had a quick retort on the tip of her tongue about inherent sexism, especially as she believed he was deliberately baiting her, but then he turned to stand beside her with his large hand pressed to the small of her back. The unexpected contact scorched her skin and stirred her very soul, and it was all she could do to remember how to walk, let alone speak.

'You look stunning, Little Doc.'

'I don't think I care for that term,' she lied, because something told her she *ought* not like it.

He waved his hand negligently. 'Apologies. You look quite lovely, *Isla.*'

She thought she preferred the previous compliment; it somehow sounded more...off-guard. And she liked the idea of unbalancing this man who was clearly accustomed to being so in-control.

'I... Thank you.' Electricity jolted through her as Nikhil lifted his hand to the small of her back again and began to usher her smoothly to the doors. 'But this isn't a date.'

She wasn't sure whether she'd intended it as a reminder to him, or to her. But, either way, she felt the first hint of disappointment when he dipped his head instantly.

'Of course not.'

It was wholly, utterly insane, the way he affected her. Surely this couldn't be normal? It certainly wasn't normal for her.

With hindsight, it was now all the more evident to Isla that she really ought to have declined his invitation to dinner. So, what did it say about her that something inside was practically elated that it was too late to back out now?

Touching her had been a mistake, Nikhil realised the moment his fingers touched her skin and a fresh bolt of awareness crackled through his entire body.

Another mistake. On top of the fact that he'd asked her to dinner in the first place.

All because he'd been thrown off-kilter by a goddamned birthday card, and it provided the escape that he needed to avoid meeting the man who he had once looked up to as his hero brother.

Back when he'd been naïve, he thought angrily, before Daksh had betrayed him so comprehensively.

It was that which had made him so edgy today. So unlike his usual unruffled self that he'd ended up inviting this woman—this stranger—to join him at his annual pilgrimage to Te Tinca. All because of a bout of plain old sexual attraction.

Except that there was nothing *plain*, or *old*,

about the attraction he felt for the unexpected doctor, was there? After all, from the moment he'd heard her shoes echoing on the marble floor and looked up to see her striding so confidently, sexily, towards him, in heels that make her calves look all the more shapely, and her backside that little bit perter, he'd felt something kick hard, low in his abdomen.

And lower still.

Sexual attraction was one thing, but he had no words for the intensity of what had arced between the two of them ever since he'd crouched down next to her, beside Philippe. And he could read women well enough to know that she felt it too.

Even tonight he'd paced his suite like some sort of caged beast, unable to stay on the ship and finding himself in the lobby of her hotel, still battling to tame this uninvited thing which roared through him.

He could put it down to the long months at sea—unlike a significant proportion of the ship, he had never indulged in the bed-hopping for which cruises were renowned. He'd prided himself that he'd always kept his career life clearly distinct from his sex life. Yet it had never left him feeling as restless, and jumpy, as he did now.

The backstreets to the restaurant were dark and

quiet, allowing the sound of her heels to click that little bit longer. His skull hurt from shutting down all the X-rated images that it kept throwing up in his mind. It felt all too intimate. As if the warm night had cleared everywhere out just for them.

He didn't want a meal, or a conversation. He just wanted to kiss her, to scratch this impossible itch that she'd caused—all over his skin. The kind of deep, unreachable, visceral itch that he didn't think he'd ever experienced before.

Nikhil locked his jaw tight and propelled them on. Desire was closing around him, as terrifyingly vast and deep as the ocean itself. Every moment he spent with this woman felt like sinking beneath the waves that little bit further. And there was nothing he could do to save himself.

Worse, there was nothing he *wanted* to do to save himself.

'You will be glad to know that Philippe is doing well,' he ground out.

As if a scrap of banal conversation could diminish the swell of need. As if it were a pinpoint of light and he was swimming back up to meet it.

'Oh. That's great.' But her voice was too thick, as if she, too, was fighting to resurface.

'Thanks, in no small part, to you.'

The silence swirled around them again. Heavy. Bewitching.

'What about your doctor? I presume you found out why he wasn't on shore where you expected him to be.'

They both pretended there wasn't desperation in her voice. That she, like him, wasn't trying to fill the silence in order to stave off this animal lust that seemed to flow through them both.

'Appendicitis,' he told her grimly. 'He'll be out for a couple of weeks, so they're flying another doctor in tomorrow.'

'How does the crew feel about having a new doctor mid-cruise?' she asked suddenly.

And, against all expectation, the tension seemed to have cranked down a notch.

Nikhil shrugged, though she wasn't looking at him, her attention focused ahead of her.

'It depends on the doctor. Fortunately, I know the guy they're flying in; I worked with him in the past, before I joined the *Queen Cassiopeia*.'

'Right,' she stated flatly. 'Makes things easier.'

'Ah, you're worried about how easy your own move will be, onto the *Jewel of Hestia*.'

She pulled a rueful face and he told himself that it didn't mean anything that he could read her so easily. It was a skill he'd acquired after

years of being an officer and reading his colleagues. Or being a kid and reading his father's
temper. It had nothing to do with *her* per se.

He wasn't entirely sure he believed that.

'You'll be fine. The *Cassiopeia* is out for
months at a time; many of the crew have been
working together for years. The *Jewel* runs
shorter cruises, and the staff and crew turn-
over is higher. It's a good ship but it's a stepping stone for promotion to bigger and better
liners, so they're well accustomed to new faces.'

'You think so?'

'Keep performing like you did today with
Philippe and they'll be only too glad to have
you as one of their doctors.'

'That's a relief.' She blew out a breath and, that
easily, the tension eased down another notch.

Maybe dinner wouldn't be so fraught, after all.

He stopped her outside a nondescript door
which no one would ever have realised was the
entrance to the restaurant of a world-renowned
chef if they hadn't known it was there, and tried
not to think about the fact that 'Little Doc Isla'
was the only woman he'd ever brought here, in
all these years.

It meant nothing, he told himself as he opened
the door and waited for her to step in ahead of

him. *And if he believed that, well...he was in more trouble than he'd realised.*

'Nikhil!' A man, clearly the maître d', even though he was dressed far more casually than Isla might have expected, made his way across the tightly packed room to embrace Nikhil in a back-slapping hug, the moment they entered. His accent was so strong that Isla could only just understand the words spoken in Chilean Spanish.

'Is good to see you back, my friend.'

'It's good to be back,' Nikhil responded in Spanish, slightly clearer to Isla, but still so full of Chilean slang that she couldn't follow as they plunged into conversation.

And then, suddenly, the chef turned to her with an unexpectedly assessing look, his English almost as heavily accented as his native language.

'You are bringing company, Nikhil?'

'Isla, this is Hernandez. Hernandez, this is Isla. A...colleague.'

'Encantada de conocerte.'

'Encantado.' He took her hand and kissed it, but Isla didn't miss the unfathomable look that passed between the two men. 'Come, I sit you both here. Best table in the housing.'

As Isla followed Hernandez, all too aware of

Nikhil right behind her, she took in some of the people at the tables. And then, as she glanced into the open kitchen beyond the pass, she startled.

'That's Chef Miguel.'

'It is,' Nikhil confirmed, with a casualness that she couldn't quite have said why she didn't believe.

'I heard his restaurants are always booked up months in advance?'

Nikhil watched her for a moment before answering. 'Six months in advance, yes. I've been coming here for seven years, every time I'm in port. So maybe two or three times a year.'

'And the Captain gives you shore leave each time?'

'In the beginning, when I was more junior, it was the only one I ever actually asked for. Otherwise, I'd take any others people didn't want.'

'Then you became First Officer and got the prime choices?'

There was something about her tone that made him pause, just for a fraction of a moment. As though she was expecting the worst. As though she expected people to be selfish.

It was the way he'd felt almost his entire life but somehow, on her, it didn't seem to fit.

'I get more choice now, it's true, but I still try to play fair.'

And what did it say about her that she believed him?

'Impressive place to bring all your dates.' She tried to keep her tone light, but it was still an attempt to counter any gullibility on her part.

'I thought we weren't on a date?'

She flushed prettily, and he liked it rather too much.

'We aren't…of course not… I meant…'

'Relax.' He grinned. 'You're the first date-but-not-a-date I've ever brought here.'

Cobalt-blue eyes slid away, narrowed, then slid back to his.

'Really? You expect me to believe that?'

'I don't expect you to do anything. But you asked, and I answered. I've never brought any date here. Save for the Captain once, a year ago, I've never brought anyone here.'

Nikhil bit down on his tongue, but it was too late. The admission was out there, although, judging by the look of disbelief on Isla's face, she didn't believe him anyway.

And that was a good thing, he told himself.

He had no idea what the heck it was about this woman that was so compelling, but he needed to work it out as soon as possible. She was like a puzzle, and he hated puzzles.

No, more accurately, he *enjoyed* puzzles; he just hated an unsolved one. And the brain-teaser that was Doc Isla was taking up far too much of his time.

So, as far as Nikhil was concerned, the sooner he solved it—*her*—the sooner normal life could resume.

CHAPTER THREE

ISLA SWALLOWED AGAIN. She wanted to show him that she didn't believe that he hadn't brought any other date here. More to the point, that it didn't matter to her even if he had.

The problem was that it *did* matter to her.

Rather too much.

An uninvited thrill rippled through her as she thought back to the look of surprise on Hernandez' face when he'd realised Nikhil had brought her as a date. That unspoken communication that had travelled between the two of them supported Nikhil's claim, and therefore made her feel all the more special.

Just like Bradley had.

Pretending that he'd cared for her, and that her money, her connections, her social standing, didn't enter into it. Briefly, she wondered if Nikhil was as straight-talking as he appeared, or if he was also the kind of man to lie, and pretend he loved a woman.

She shook the thoughts from her head irritably. Why did everything have to lead back to Bradley? Even now, months and months later, she was still giving him the power to dominate her thoughts, her actions. And she was furious with herself for doing so.

He was in her past.

Gone.

She didn't want to think about him any more.

'You said the *Hestia* was to be your first cruise?'

Isla blinked and looked up to realise that they'd been sitting in silence for so long she'd finished her course without even realising it.

'I've been a doctor for ten years, but this will be the first time I've been a doctor for a cruise ship,' she offered eventually.

'Ten years?' He didn't look convinced. 'Doctors are qualifying in their teens now, Little Doc?'

'I'm thirty-two.' She fought to keep her voice even.

She'd faced bigger slights than that. There was no reason for it to cut any deeper simply because it came from this man.

'I didn't realise.' His expression changed. 'Still, you must have worked hard to graduate at twenty-two.'

She had—not least because people had wanted

to doubt her. Because of her age. And because of who her previous stepfather had been.

But although Stefan Claybourne had been one of the best stepfathers she'd ever known, and he'd certainly encouraged her dream to become a doctor, his kindness and support hadn't been a substitute for her own hard work.

'Being a doctor is all I've ever wanted to do.' She shrugged instead. 'Even as a child, I dreamed of it when other kids were dreaming of being princesses or pirates.'

'Doesn't make the work any easier.'

'No,' she conceded, 'it doesn't. But it does mean that the hard work has always been worth it. Then again, you must know that. You don't get to First Officer on a line like the *Queen Cassiopeia* without being equally dedicated to what you do.'

'For me it was a way out. It was never a dream.'

Isla turned her head sharply to look at him. She wasn't sure which of them was more surprised at the revelation.

'A way out?'

He didn't answer for a long time.

'Where I came from there weren't many choices in life. Maritime was one of them, and so I decided if I was going to go into that, then

I wasn't going to be in some hot, stinking job in the bowels of a ship.'

'I think that makes what you've achieved all the more impressive.' She swallowed.

It was impossible to shake the hunch that he wasn't the kind of man who was usually this open with people. Then again, what did she know? Bradley had been a terrible liar, and yet she'd never thought to question him. Because she'd believed—contrary to everything her mother's carefully negotiated marriages had taught her—that true love really did exist.

Nikhil could just be incredibly skilled at making people—*women*—believe that he was revealing some hitherto unknown facet of himself. At making a woman feel special.

But she wasn't that stupid. What did they say about fooling a person once…?

So then, what are you doing here? a silent voice taunted her.

Isla stifled it quickly. She didn't want to hear what it had to say.

'What about your parents? They must be proud.'

'My parents are both dead.'

There was nothing emotional about the admission; a casual observer would have thought it factual, with an even and calm delivery. Yet

Isla thought that something altogether bleaker flashed through his eyes for a fraction of a moment.

Then it was gone, leaving her wondering if she'd merely imagined it.

'Oh—' she scrambled for the appropriate response '—I'm sorry.'

'It happened a long time ago.'

Nikhil shrugged, but she didn't know if that made it better or worse. But then Hernandez came with another course from the tasting menu, and Isla found herself fascinated by the dish. Such a precise, delicate-looking creation that should surely have been more at home in an art gallery but which, when tasted, exploded in her mouth like the most perfect taste she'd ever known.

'Impressive, isn't it?' Nikhil asked.

'Incredible,' she breathed. 'Is this always what you have? I can see why you come back every time you can.'

'No, it's always a different tasting menu for me. And every time I think it can't possibly get any better. Yet it does.'

For several more minutes they tasted and praised, and Isla didn't know how it had happened but the last of her disquiet seemed to have eased.

'So the *Hestia* is to be your new start?'

He jerked his head down and she was once again reminded of her now bare ring finger, giving her away without her even speaking a word. She pasted a bright smile onto her lips.

'Yes, it's a good career move. A chance for me to concentrate on being a doctor, with no distractions.'

His deep bark of laughter, rich and full-bodied, filled her with something new.

'You're not serious?'

'I am.' She frowned. 'What's wrong with that?'

'This is a cruise ship you're going on.' He laughed again, and suddenly she wished she could bottle it up and take it with her.

She didn't know why.

'I know it's a cruise ship. And I'm a doctor.'

'You're a stunning, educated, newly single doctor,' he corrected. 'And you must know the reputation cruise ships have for bed-hopping. Among staff just as much as among the passengers. Sometimes even more so.'

It was insane how his words instantly threw out a series of images of Nikhil bed-hopping. And even more insane how her body balked against them. As if it actually mattered to her.

'I thought you said you didn't bed-hop.' She tried not to sound so prim, but failed.

'I never mentioned my private life on board.' He arched his eyebrows, giving her the oddest impression that he could read her every naughty thought. 'I merely said I'd never brought a date to this restaurant.'

Fire scorched through her cheeks. 'Oh.'

'But, for what it's worth, I don't.' She didn't know why he'd suddenly relented. 'I try to keep my private life quite distinct from my role as ship's officer.'

It said rather too much, in Isla's mind, that they were the words she'd wanted to hear. She straightened her shoulders. 'As I intend to do.'

He laughed again. 'The difference is, Little Doc, that you're already inviting speculation the moment they see that faded mark around your finger.'

'Well, I won't answer it.'

'You'll have to; they won't let it go because it's too juicy a story. The heartbroken new doc.'

'I don't want to be a juicy story, and I'm not heartbroken.'

'Aren't you?' He sounded genuinely curious. 'Your engagement has broken down and suddenly you're a doctor on a cruise ship heading around the world. Like you're running away.'

Indignation fired up her spine. 'I'm not running away.'

Was she?

'Is that so?' he asked, then lifted his shoulders. 'Well, ships are such odd environments. Some might say we're tight-knit cities, others would say we're just living in each other's pockets. Either way, there are never really any secrets, and people are always in everyone else's business.'

'Meaning?'

'Meaning that I can already see some well-meaning colleagues trying to set you up with all and sundry, just to get you over your heartbreak.'

'I told you…'

'You're not heartbroken,' he finished. 'Yes, I heard. But I don't imagine that will stop them.'

'God, that's just like my mother.' Isla rolled her eyes. 'She's equally well-intentioned, but it doesn't make it any less irritating. She's always on about me having a rebound fling. If I hadn't told her that I was on a date with a First Officer, then she already had a blind date set up for me.'

If he was surprised that she'd suddenly mentioned her mother when she'd told him that afternoon that she was with friends then he didn't show it.

'So you're only with me to dodge your mother? I'm flattered,' he drawled, not looking in the least concerned. 'Anyway, I thought this wasn't a date?'

'Is isn't.' She stumbled over her words.

Why did she keep making that mistake?

'Shame—' another wicked smile played on his lips, toying with them and simultaneously pulling at something low in her belly '—I don't think I'd have minded you using me to get over whoever he was.'

Desire seeped through her. At this point she wasn't entirely sure she'd have minded that either.

'Anyway...' she began, trying to change the subject before her mind went blank.

She was almost relieved when Hernandez came with the next course of the tasting menu.

'Wow, this smells incredible.'

'Doesn't it?' he agreed. 'But be aware that Chef Miguel likes to play with the senses. Whatever you think you're getting, be prepared for it to catch you out.'

Nodding slowly, Isla loaded a careful amount onto her fork and lifted it to her mouth. Taste and sensation exploded in her mouth and, just as Nikhil had predicted, it challenged her expectations of what she'd thought she'd smelled.

'That's amazing. He's really brilliant.'

'He is. And, like I said, he's always evolving and inventing.'

'I guess I'm going to have to come back and

see for myself.' She grinned, and then felt a jolt. 'I mean…by myself. I'm not… That wasn't…'

'Relax, I understand what you meant,' Nikhil cut in. 'I take it your mother would rather have you be a private practice doctor than travelling around the world on a cruise ship?'

'My mother would rather I not be a doctor at all,' Isla admitted before thinking twice, as Nikhil pulled his brows together.

'Really? She isn't proud of you?'

Was it just her imagination, or did she detect a note of…*something* in his tone?

'Sorry, that isn't fair.' She wrinkled her nose. 'My mother is always proud. Although she doesn't really understand why it's my dream.'

'Why not?'

She paused; this wasn't usually a conversation she had with strangers. Or many people, in fact. But, rather than push her, Nikhil waited, his eyes never leaving hers. So different from the way Bradley had always been far more interested in who he could see, who could see him, what was on his phone.

It was potent to have Nikhil's attention so assuredly on her. As if nothing else mattered to him but whatever she was saying. It almost had her telling him things that she rarely told anyone.

Isla just about caught herself in time and moderated what she'd been about to say.

'My mother can't see the appeal of actually working in the trenches with blood, and vomit, and sick people. Her philosophy is that she can contribute more by marrying well, playing her role, organising fundraisers and raising millions, which she then gives to hospitals and charities.'

'And your father?'

'My father died when I was two. I have photos though I don't remember him. But I had a surgeon stepfather, Stefan, when I was fourteen.' No need to tell him she'd had five stepfathers so far. 'He encouraged me to follow my dream and go into medicine.'

'He was kind?' asked Nikhil, too sharply and too quickly.

Had he had his own, less fortunate experiences with a stepfather? Stepmother?

'He was very kind. I was lucky.' Isla smiled softly.

None of her stepfathers had ever been unkind; her mother would never have married them otherwise. But Stefan had been like the father she'd never known.

'He even had a daughter, Leonora, who was about the same age as me. She didn't want to go into medicine. In fact she wanted to be an art-

ist and she could paint the most stunning paint-
ings, and he always encouraged her too. There
was never any favour to either of us. He treated
us both like we were his daughters.'

'You speak of it in the past,' Nikhil pointed out.

'Yeah, their marriage—business agreement—
ended when I was nineteen, though Stefan came
to see me a couple of times at the hospital where
I did my first few rotations. But Leo and I are
still best friends. We're each the sister the other
never had.'

'It sounds very…civilised,' Nikhil commented.

She might have said *through gritted teeth* if she
hadn't thought better of it. Instead, she laughed
quietly.

'Civility is my mother's mantra. What about
you? You don't have any siblings?'

It took him a beat too long to answer and, when
he did, it struck Isla as an incredibly telling and
personal statement.

'I have a brother. But I lost him a long time
ago.'

'I'm sorry to hear that,' she offered genuinely.
The thought of losing Leo wasn't one she wanted
to even consider. 'You must miss him.'

'Not really,' Nikhil replied instantly.

But, despite his attempt at a casual tone, Isla
couldn't help thinking she saw something deeper,

more genuine, usually hidden. Something profoundly sad. Though perhaps she was just being fanciful.

As if he was going to show her a side of himself that no one else ever saw.

'My brother wasn't what you might call the dependable sort. Most people aren't, which is why I can understand why your mother doesn't believe in love.'

Guilt lanced through Isla.

'My mother might not believe in *love* as some deep, romantic concept, but she definitely believes in love for me as her daughter,' she said, almost apologetically. 'And for Leo, come to that. Even now, she still treats Leo like another daughter. If she phones me to see how I am, she will have either called, or be about to call Leo too. If she buys me something, she buys something for Leo.'

'You don't resent that?'

'It makes me feel as though we're still family. In fact, when I told you before that I was here with friends, I wasn't being entirely truthful. My mother flew herself and Leo out yesterday as a surprise. And, as you surmised, we're going for dinner together tomorrow night. Though she'll be furious she didn't book here. That's her idea of love.'

'Indeed.' Nikhil offered a half-smile but didn't elaborate. Instead, he turned his questions back on her. 'And what about you? Do you believe in love?'

Isla hesitated. She had done. Once upon a time.

For all her mother's wisdom and lessons, she'd believed that true love—soulmates—had to exist, somewhere. A thousand blockbuster romantic films couldn't be wrong. And when she'd fallen for Bradley she'd understood what every single one of them meant.

Or she'd *thought* she'd understood.

'Not any more,' she told Nikhil simply, quashing the traitorous part of her that tried to argue. 'You?'

'Never,' he answered.

And she thought it was the fact that it was said so certainly, with no emotion or heat, that made it all the more...*lamentable.*

'Are you always so controlled? Don't you ever feel passionate about anything?'

It was a foolish question. She realised it at exactly the same moment that his eyes darkened, his expression walloping her like a punch to the solar plexus—only far, far more exhilarating.

'I might only be able to offer one night, Little Doc, but I can show plenty of passion, if that's what you want.'

The heat, the intensity, that she'd felt earlier now felt more like a wall. And she was racing straight for it.

'Not a date,' she managed weakly.

'Of course not,' he agreed with a smile that she could swear she could actually feel against her sex. 'But if you feel yourself wavering, just let me know.'

'Right,' she murmured. Unable to even deny it.

The wall was approaching faster now.

If she wasn't careful, she was going to crash—and that could only hurt.

It was several hours before they left the restaurant. The last to leave, after being served one incredible dish after another, and even Chef Miguel had left the kitchen to come and sit with them for after-dinner drinks, chatting with Nikhil as though they were old friends.

Clearly they were.

But whilst Brad would have preened and peacocked, making her cringe a little at his sycophantism—the way that he always had when Isla had taken him to one of her mother's high-society events—Nikhil kept it all comfortable and easy.

It told her a lot more about him. And she liked what she saw.

But now it was just the two of them. Her and Nikhil, in the quiet, narrow back streets, which were glowing faintly from the warm yellow-orange lights spilling out from the buildings on either side.

His arm was around her, almost protectively, and she was wholly conscious of fitting far too well to the shape of his body. *As if they were designed to fit together.* He moved with such grace, propelling them on, with every step taking them closer and closer to her hotel.

To end the night? Or to begin it?

Her head was warring with the rest of her body, as everything started to pull gradually tighter and tighter. It pooled in her chest, her belly, and lower. She ought to speak. To stop this. One-night stands weren't her thing, but lord, the temptation to stay silent and simply indulge in the moment made her mouth dry up completely.

In the end, it was her legs that stopped her. Slowing her down, as though against her will.

'What if I've changed my mind?'

'Changed your mind?' he asked, stopping beside her, his arm still around her waist.

Still making her blood fizz and her head spin.

'This,' Isla managed. 'Us. You said it yourself. When I go onto the *Hestia* I'll be the heartbroken girl with a broken engagement who

needs fixing. They'll all be telling me I need a rebound…unless I can tell them I've already had my rebound.'

Isla ignored the voice whispering that if she felt that was a solution then she could still pretend that she'd had a rebound without actually having one. She prayed that Nikhil wouldn't point it out either.

She wanted this one night. It would put what had happened with Bradley firmly in the past. Drawing a line between that life and this new one on the *Hestia.* Perhaps she really did need it.

Although she didn't care to analyse the fact that no other man had made her want to do something so uncharacteristic—only Nikhil.

'I don't have anything else to offer,' he said quietly, as she wondered if she imagined that tinge of regret.

'I know.'

'Be sure, Little Doc, because I'm not in the habit of talking a woman into a situation she might later regret.'

'The perfect officer and gentleman,' she quipped, wondering why he wasn't kissing her already.

He was trying to make sure she had really considered it and, as gentlemanly as that was, it left her with a faint afternote of disappointment rather than relief.

And then his voice grew edgier. Raw. 'I'm an officer but I've never been a gentleman.'

'Good, then maybe you can start by being a little less gentlemanly now.' She didn't know what had got into her, but her mouth seemed to run away with itself, egged on by more carnal parts of her body.

His eyes gleamed in the faint yellow-orange light and a kind of reckless desire poured through her, making her stomach clench—in a good way. Impulsively, she stepped forward, reached up and pressed her lips to his—finally, *finally* kissing him.

And in that incredible moment it felt as though her whole life was turning on its axis.

CHAPTER FOUR

NIKHIL COULDN'T HELP himself any longer. Or, more aptly, he didn't want to, not now Isla had initiated their kiss. It was perhaps the hottest thing he could recall experiencing.

He pressed her into the wall until every last inch of her delectable body, with all the delicious heat spilling out of it, was pressed against every last inch of his. And he lowered his mouth to her neck, and indulged. As if he couldn't help himself.

Perhaps he couldn't.

Never, in all his years, had Nikhil ever felt so hollow, and needy, and raw. As if he'd die if he didn't have her. If he didn't bury himself inside her. Right here. Right now. He, who prided himself on never losing control.

Not since that bleak, black night less than some twenty-odd years ago when, his body black and blue, his ribs cracked, his face bleeding, he'd finally stopped cowering to that monster who'd had no right to ever call himself a father. He'd unfolded himself from a heap on the floor and he'd shown that demon what it really felt like to be a punchbag.

Not that he could remember a moment of it.

To this day, Nikhil still didn't remember the moment when he'd actually killed his pathetic excuse for a father. He had, of course, because there was no other explanation. Yet he couldn't remember it. He remembered his father raging, and he remembered wresting the knife from his father's hands…but then it all went hazy, and the only thing he could remember was being led out of the apartment by a sympathetic policeman whilst they'd put his father in a body bag.

So what other explanation could there be?

And now he had that damned birthday card to deal with. Nikhil shook the unwelcome memories from his brain.

Tonight wasn't about revisiting his grubby past. Instead, tonight was about indulging in the unexpected seduction of this moment. And the temptation that was Isla. He intended to learn every millimetre of her oh-so-sensuous body. With his hands, his mouth, his tongue. He didn't care which.

Though preferably all three.

He wanted to touch her and taste her. *Lord, how he wanted to taste her.* He wanted to drink her in as though he were a parched man and she was his oasis.

'One night, Little Doc,' he heard himself grind out, scarcely able to lift his head from her neck. So hot, so smooth, with the faintest tang of salt in the still-hot night.

'Yes,' she muttered, arching her body into him and letting her head tip back as if to grant him better access. As if half-afraid he was going to move away.

'That means no recriminations once the morning comes,' he repeated, only he wasn't sure who he was reminding. Her? Or himself?

'I'm well aware of what it means.' She yanked her head up abruptly and scowled at him. 'I'm not a gullible teenage girl. But I can't control your morning tantrums.'

'No, I meant you...' It took him a moment to realise that she was teasing him. Playing him at his own game. He rather liked that. It was like a fresh kick of desire in his gut. Lower, if he was going to be honest.

'Don't say I didn't warn you,' he growled, lowering his head back to that sensitive hollow at the base of her neck—where she seemed to like him the most.

So far.

'You should learn to stop talking,' gasped Isla,

slicking her fingers through his hair just rough enough. 'One might think you're overcompensating.'

'Say again?'

He lifted his head again, though he still kept her pinned to the wall with his body.

'You're building yourself up to be God's gift,' she continued, though he noted with some satisfaction that she couldn't keep the desire from thickening her voice. 'It would be a terrible disappointment to discover your mouth is making promises that your body can't deliver.'

Was she seriously questioning his prowess?

'Oh, believe me, my body can deliver.'

'So your mouth keeps saying—' she heaved a deliberate sigh, and the shakiness of it shot through him all the more '—but your body...'

'Trust me, Little Doc, my mouth can deliver too.'

'Sorry?' This time it was her turn to question.

Just as he'd intended. He shot a smile that felt infinitely wolfish.

'My body can deliver. And so can my mouth.'

She stared at him for a moment, and then a deep stain spread over her cheeks and down the elegant line of her neck.

'Oh...you mean...'

'I intend to eat you alive, Little Doc. Until you sob my name.'

'I won't sob your name.'

He wasn't sure if that was meant to be a promise or a challenge. He found he didn't care.

'You will,' he assured her with conviction. 'And you won't only sob it, but you'll shout it, and you'll scream it. Right before you beg me for more. And more again. I intend to make absolutely sure of that.'

She made a delicious half-strangled sound, and he asked himself what it said about him that he wondered if that was the kind of sound he would hear again and again, as she broke apart in his arms.

He was so hard that he ached. Barely able to resist the wicked urge to drop to his knees right here, lift that flimsy dress of hers and prove his point once and for all.

If he wasn't careful, he risked losing the last of his grip on some semblance of self-control. With a supreme effort, Nikhil peeled his body from Isla's, took her hand and began to walk them down the street.

'Come,' he gritted out. 'I suggest we get back to your hotel now, before we indulge in the middle of the street and embarrass both of us.'

Although, for the very first time in his incredibly discreet professional life, Nikhil found he wouldn't have cared if the whole city knew that Little Doc was his.

Even if only for this one night.

Isla felt crazy. Wild. Out of control. Totally unlike herself.

And it was so freeing.

She'd spent her life trying to be different from her mother—as much as she loved her—trying to concentrate on her career rather than simply making a series of strategic marriages.

She'd become known as Isla, the sensible one. And she'd prided herself on such a moniker.

But now she didn't feel sensible at all. She felt excited, and charged, and feverish. Her heart slammed madly in her chest. Her legs trembled like a newborn foal. And, far from terrifying her, as she suspected they ought to, they instead felt like truly joyous sensations. Every last one of them.

She hurried along beside him, trying not to be so aware of the way his large hand enveloped her small one. Or how the *click-clack* of her heels seemed to echo with such titillating rudeness as she raced to keep up with his long strides. As though he could barely wait any longer than she could.

Did he feel as though he was about to burst from the inside out, the way that she did?

They moved swiftly through the narrow streets, with Nikhil weaving a path that kept them away from the melee of tourists, sparing them from being seen. Given that she suspected her desire was stamped blatantly on her face, Isla was eternally grateful. And then they were walking through the hotel doors.

And upstairs was her bedroom.

'Key card?' he demanded, his voice low.

'In my purse.' She licked her suddenly parched lips.

With a nod, he changed course slightly and made straight for the elevators on the far side where one was, mercifully, already there.

An elderly couple were already stepping inside and Nikhil slowed his pace.

'Which floor?'

To her embarrassment, her mind went blank. Nikhil's voice was hoarser than before, and she found herself too busy savouring the way it revealed more than she suspected he would have liked.

'What floor, Isla?' he repeated, with more urgency.

Snapping back to the present, she shook her head before fumbling with the clasp of her clutch and fishing out her key card. She handed it to him discreetly, not trusting herself, and let him lead her forward for what felt the longest elevator-ride of her life.

How did he manage, so easily, to respond as the elderly couple made pleasant conversation, when her own tongue felt as though it was glued to the roof of her mouth? Her body might as well have been on fire, and her brain could barely process their questions let alone formulate suitable responses. Yet Nikhil seemed more than comfortable engaging in small talk and suggesting some of the more tucked-away places to visit when they asked for his advice.

It was only as they stood outside her tiny suite, the doors pinging behind them as it finally separated them from the elderly couple, that Nikhil handed her key card back to her. Without unlocking her door.

She stared at the tiny rectangle of plastic without taking it, and frowned up at him. 'You've changed your mind?'

Coal-black eyes bored into her, making everything tingle all over again. 'I have not.' His voice was a low rumble. Full of promise. And barely contained restraint. 'But I'm giving you one more chance to change yours.'

Something like panic shot through her. 'Why?'

He lifted his shoulders. Not quite a shrug, but close enough. 'You went so quiet in the lift. I thought you were having second thoughts.'

A wave of relief crashed over her, and the panic was swept away in an instant. She struggled to contain the grin as it tugged at the corners of her mouth. And with it came a welcome boost of confidence.

Extending her fingers, Isla plucked the key card from his hand and slid it home, stepping over the threshold and turning to face him. Her hands lifting up until her palms were pressed against the warm, impossibly sculpted ridges of his chest.

Moving over them.

Acquainting herself with them.

'I wasn't,' she murmured, raising herself on tiptoe and letting her lips graze his. 'I didn't change my mind for a moment. And I don't intend to now.'

Then, before he could answer, she closed her fists around his lapels and tugged him off balance, right over the threshold to her room.

Nikhil fully intended to take his time. To taste, to sample, to tend to Isla's needs before he even began to think about his own. But, uncharacteristically, he found she'd caught him off-guard, his wondrous 'Little Doc', and he found himself fighting his own urgency.

No other woman had ever made him feel so intoxicated. So possessed.

Stumbling inside, he managed to close the door before spinning her around so that her back was against the door, his hands exploring her ravishing body.

And she let him. She more than let him, she actively spurred him on, wrapping her arms around his neck and fitting herself to him. Moulding herself as though she were hand-crafted—*just for him*. The prospect should have been enough to set off warning bells, loud and clear, in his head.

He deliberately didn't stop to consider the fact that it hadn't.

Instead, Nikhil focused his entire thoughts on lowering his head to claim her mouth with his. Hot, demanding, hungry. From the slide of her lips to the slick of his tongue, all of which elicited from her the greediest little moans of approval, and all of which his body lapped up.

He didn't think he'd ever been so hard, so *needy* his entire life. How had this woman slid under his skin? It was ridiculous. He had to slow down.

Setting one hand against the flimsy door beside her head, Nikhil slid the other down the side of her body, letting it curve around her waist, feeling her heat seep into him. His mouth never leaving hers. Slowly, he moved his fingers, a teasing caress, walking his way across her abdomen, not quite enough to tickle, but feeling her stomach clench sensitively nonetheless.

Anticipation. Usually, he was all about it. All about the build-up. Today, with this woman, it was taking every bit of self-control he had not to simply rip her clothes off and bury himself inside her. The way her rocking body kept urging him on was enough to drive him out of his mind. Enough to make him forget he'd ever wanted any other woman in his life before her.

He'd certainly never wanted them with this ferocity. And still she shifted and rolled her hips. Searing heat against the hardest part of himself.

He made himself ignore it, though he had no idea how he managed it, choosing instead to concentrate on the feel of movement of her diaphragm beneath his hands as she breathed. Heavily, he noted with satisfaction. He took his time walking his fingers a little further, a little higher, and then he was pushing her bra aside and cupping her breast in his hand, testing it, letting his thumb pad rake over her hard, proud nipple.

The urge to lower his head and take it in his mouth was overwhelming. And so he did. Tugging the flimsy material of the dress and the lace of the bra out of the way as he did.

Isla gasped, her fingers raking through his hair and her head dropping back. Nikhil revelled in it. She tasted of pure desire. Ripe and unrestrained, and as Nikhil used his tongue to toy with the taut peak he couldn't resist moving his hand to free her other breast from its fabric constraints and lavish upon it an equal amount of attention.

The world seemed to stop, or maybe it spun faster, but he refused to be hurried. He might be teetering on the edge of control, but he'd be damned if he gave in to this overwhelming, aching desire for her, until he'd brought her pleasure first.

Brushing his hand over her body, down her belly and to the hem of her skirt, he lifted it with a forced laziness, relishing the way Isla's breath caught, and fractured.

And then, so slowly, he grazed his fingers up the inside of her thigh and skimmed where she was so very hot, so very wet, that it was almost his undoing. He was so hard, so aching, that it was almost like pain, and he had no idea how he managed not to simply bury himself inside her.

* * *

Isla was going out of her mind. She was sure of it.

She briefly wondered how Nikhil kept his control when she'd long since lost hers, but then he hooked his finger inside her panties and stroked her core, and she ignited. Over and over he stroked her, and she couldn't speak, couldn't think. It was like nothing that had ever gone before.

Instead, lost between his mouth at her neck and his fingers on her sex, she simply let her body listen to the rhythm that he was setting. Meeting it. Matching it. And surely those needy, visceral noises couldn't possibly be her?

Still, he kept stroking her. Over and over, like the most exquisite kind of torture, driving her onward, and upward, until she realised—almost too late—that she was toppling over the edge.

Isla just about managed to cling to Nikhil's strong shoulders as she fell. Hurtling weightlessly, pleasure fragmenting around her. And she had absolutely no idea how long she fell, she was only vaguely aware of holding him tightly—as if afraid that if she let go he would disappear—as he wrapped her legs around his waist, and carried her to the huge bed in the middle of the room.

She could only watch, spellbound, as he stripped her off. And then again, as he ruthlessly shed his own clothing. Naked, hard, and clearly ready for her. Undoubtedly the most beautiful man she'd ever known in her life.

Isla reached for him.

'What's the rush, Little Doc?' he drawled.

But she heard the tightness in his tone, as though he wasn't quite as restrained as he wanted to appear. It was a thrilling notion and one which she considered exploiting—right up until she watched him lodge himself between her legs, his mouth impossibly close to where she was already molten.

'I don't think I can again...' she whispered shakily.

There was no other way to describe his grin but as decidedly wicked.

'I disagree,' he murmured.

Then, before she could add anything more, he lowered his head and licked his way into her.

She screamed his name. It was impossible not to. And somehow her hands had made their way to his head as she threaded her fingers into his hair as if to give herself better purchase as she bucked her hips beneath him. Towards him.

As if she was utterly incapable of doing any-thing less.

As if he had completely taken over her. And she couldn't have resisted, even if she'd wanted to.

Was this what she'd been missing? All these years? It made a mockery of everything that had gone before. Had she really been happy to settle for less with Bradley—and not even realised it?

For the first time, Isla felt as though her eyes had been opened. She felt alive. In a rush, she realised that, as transient as tonight would be, she would always remember Nikhil for showing her how much richer her life could be.

And then she couldn't think any more.

She could only feel, as he used his mouth, his fingers, weaving some kind of spell around her, more carnal than she'd ever dreamed possible. With another sweep of his tongue he toppled her straight back into the flames, and she briefly considered that even if she burned alive she wouldn't care.

She bucked, and she let her hips roll. And this time when she gave herself up to him, breaking, splintering, she somehow knew that this was the way she was going to make herself anew.

And for the first time in her life Isla let herself go completely.

By the time she came to, Nikhil had moved his body up to cover hers, carefully and gently, as though to give her time to regain her breath.

Nonetheless the evidence of his desire pressed deliciously, like velvety steel, against her belly.

Isla ran her hands over his body, taking it all in. From the knotted muscles of his back, to strong biceps, and then the solid bulk of his shoulders. She frowned slightly at the rough scar that adorned one of them. It was old, but it caught her doctor's eye instantly.

'What was this from?'

She hated the way his eyes shuttered on her.

'Old war wound, as they say.'

'It looks like a knife wound. A deep one at that.'

His eyes held hers. So intently that she almost forgot to breathe. And she didn't know why it was so important to her, but she found herself urging him to talk to her. Not to shut her out again.

'We're not here for story-telling, Little Doc. We don't have to share life stories.'

Disappointment rolled through her, but she pasted on as much of a smile as she could.

'I only asked what the scar was from. I wasn't asking for your life story, Nikhil.'

He watched her a little longer before offering an almost imperceptible dip of his head.

'You're right; it was a knife wound,' he confirmed. 'A kitchen accident with a carving knife. Does that satisfy your curiosity?'

She wanted to say that it didn't. That she hated the way he was pulling away from her. But she didn't. She couldn't. Nikhil was right. They weren't here to share life stories; they were here for sex. Incredible sex. But still sex. She was an idiot for making it so personal. And now she'd broken the moment, and the mood.

She cranked up her smile another notch.

'Completely satisfied,' she lied, wondering how best to extricate herself from such an intimate position without making things all the more awkward.

At least her answer seemed to have eased the tension slightly.

'You're sure?' he asked suddenly. 'Completely satisfied?'

And then he flexed against her and Isla marvelled at how the awkwardness dissipated in an instant. As though there was no room for it when her desire came cannoning back.

'You think you can do better?' she teased after a moment.

His eyebrows shot up, and she liked that she had finally found a way to tease him back.

'A challenge, Little Doc?'

'A gauntlet.' She grinned, only for it to fade into

a low gasp as he shifted, pressing her legs apart again and nudging at her entrance.

She slid her hands to his back, almost in readiness as he held himself steady, poised above her.

'Then allow me to defend my honour,' he growled.

And, before she could answer, he thrust inside her. Deep, and big, and perfect. Isla cried out, low and wanton, her back arching up and sensation seeping all around her body. Nikhil slid out slowly, almost teasing her, and she opened her eyes to meet the cocoa-rich depths of his, seeing the same intense, primal expression that echoed inside her. Something walloped inside her chest but she didn't care to examine it any further.

Instead she simply gave herself up to the sensations, letting Nikhil drive the rhythm and matching him stroke for stroke, her fingers biting into the strong cords of muscles at his neck. And then she felt the wave cresting over her. That blissful shiver pouring straight through her.

'Stop fighting it,' he growled.

Low and raw, into that crook of her neck. Making her tremble.

'I'm not fighting,' she countered.

But maybe she was. Maybe she never wanted this moment, this feverish need, to end. What if this was the only time she would ever know something this good?

As if reading her thoughts, Nikhil lifted his head, his eyes boring straight into her.

'We have all night, Little Doc. And I intend to make use of every last minute of it.'

Then, before she could answer, he slid his hand between them. Down. Right to the centre of her need. And he played with her.

It was too much, and it was perfect.

It was as though Isla's entire world was imploding.

She was catapulted into space. Into oblivion. The most glorious ride that anyone had surely ever known. All she could do was hold on tightly, and sob out his name—just as he'd predicted.

She soared for miles. For ever. And when she finally began to return to herself she realised he was waiting for her, his face taut with his own need, lifting her legs to wrap around him, as though it could pull him in deeper.

A shudder tore through him in an instant as he gripped her closer, building that pace back up. Faster now, harder, and more demanding. Grazing her fingers down his back, she cupped his backside, urging him on with such abandon that she barely recognised herself.

A bolder side of herself that she'd never realised had lurked within. She rather thought she liked it.

Then Nikhil thrust into her one last time, deep and true, and she couldn't think any more. She just wanted to *experience* everything that this arresting man had to teach her.

And this time, when Nikhil tossed her back into that glorious abyss, he followed, her name never sounding more beautiful on his lips.

CHAPTER FIVE

'HIS NAME IS JALEEL,' the security officer explained as he hastily led Isla down a rabbit warren of corridors to the ship's laundry room.

And not the *Hestia*, as had been planned, right up until the phone call from Head Office that morning—less than an hour after Nikhil had left her bed, and her hotel—but on the *Cassiopeia* itself.

She could only imagine how furious he would be when he discovered her here—if he hadn't already been advised. Goosebumps prickled over her skin at the mere thought.

But there was no time to think about that now. She'd been in the middle of her orientation tour with her new medical team when the medical call had come in, and now she had *Jaleel* to concentrate on.

Talk about being thrown in at the deep end.

'His colleague said that he stood up when there was an open machine door above him and it cut his face,' the security guard continued.

'My report said that he's unconscious,' Isla stated, adrenalin pumping through her body.

'Yeah, apparently he fell back, and they heard him cry out, and then he hit his head and fell unconscious.'

'Understood. And it's Jaleel?'

'Jaleel, yeah.'

She'd barely stepped on board—she had only just met the first of her colleagues, a stunning American nurse by the name of Jordanna—when the call had come in.

The senior doctor—a Dr Turner, according to her email—had been in his consultation room with a patient when she'd arrived. And though he could probably have taken the emergency call, Isla knew that his priority would be passengers, whilst hers, as junior doctor, would be crew and staff. There would be some crossover, of course, but in broad terms that was how this ship worked, and the sooner she jumped into that, the better she would be likely to fit in.

Finally arriving at the laundry room, Isla ducked inside and quickly took in the scene. The patient, Jaleel, was now conscious and clutching a blood-soaked towel to his face. Even from here, it looked like he was a mess, not helped by the sapping heat of the loud, airless room.

'Hi, Jaleel—' she flashed her brightest, most

confident smile '—I'm Isla, the new doctor. Let's have a look at the damage, shall we?'

'He no speak English,' the woman offered, before appearing to translate.

'Thank you.' Isla flashed her a smile as she crouched down beside Jaleel. She carefully helped him to peel the towel away and peered at the wound, then stood up.

'Which machine?'

'This…' A young woman stepped forward. 'This machine.'

Isla inspected it carefully, looking for the likely metal culprit.

'Is this where you caught it, Jaleel?'

She didn't really need to hear them say it; the blood was evidence enough. Still there was a quick exchange between the two colleagues before the woman issued a confirmation.

'Okay, good.' She crouched back down to check his vitals, shining a light into his eyes to check pupil responses.

Ideally a CT would check that he hadn't hit his head when he'd fallen backwards, but that wasn't possible on board. Still, nothing jumped out at her as a cause for alarm, save for the one long, ugly gash running down his cheek.

'It's too deep to simply glue the sides together, so let's get him back to the med centre, where

I can stitch him back up,' she told the security guard, before turning back to Jaleel's colleague. 'How long was he out, do you know?'

'Out?'

'Sorry, unconscious.'

'Oh…maybe one minute? Maybe two?'

So, not long. That was good. Nonetheless, it would be safer to transport him on the emergency gurney that they'd brought. Quickly, she set it up next to Jaleel and popped a collar around his neck for stability. She didn't think he'd injured it in the fall, but until they got him back to the medical centre it wouldn't hurt to take precautions.

'Okay, gentlemen—' she lifted her head to the security guys, who were also around the stretcher '—one, two, three, lift. Good. Now, let's get him to the medical centre.'

Jordanna was bustling around quickly and efficiently as Isla arrived in the medical centre, its location in the passenger area of the ship evident as they left behind the cold grey metal and vinyl floor of the crew decks and stepped into the pristine white-walled and plushly carpeted passenger areas.

This time Dr Turner could be seen behind his desk, his consultation door open. He was an older gentleman dressed in an immaculate uniform, and out of the corner of her eye Isla was aware that he'd stood up as soon as she'd entered with Jaleel.

She kept her focus on her patient. No doubt the medical team would all be a little uncertain of her, as a new arrival, but the better she performed here, the quicker she proved herself as a valuable member of the team.

'Jordanna, can you go ahead and ready some gauze swabs to staunch the bleeding once I remove this towel from Jaleel's face, and a suture kit, please?'

'Sure, Dr Sinclair.'

'And some local anaesthetic,' added Isla.

She busied herself checking over Jaleel's neck once more, before she finally removed the collar. Then, as Jordanna laid out all the equipment for her, she glanced at Jaleel's colleague and smiled gently.

'Can you warn him that the needle will need to go as close to the edges of the wound as possible, so it's going to be uncomfortable?'

She waited for Jaleel to nod his confirmation, and then she lifted the syringe.

'Okay, here we go.'

A few moments later, as the anaesthetic began to kick in, she picked up a small probe.

'I just want to check there is no debris in there. No metal from the machine or anything. He might feel his cheek moving elsewhere, but he won't feel any pain.'

As his friend translated, Jaleel gave them both a weak nod. It occurred to Isla that a significant proportion of his—and his friend's—anxiety might have more to do with the fact that he wanted to get back to work. It was widely acknowledged that the laundry was one of the locations on the ship where sickness was least tolerated.

Picking up the needle and sutures, Isla began one tiny stitch after another, working slowly and methodically to draw the edges of the wound together, trying to make it as neat and unobtrusive as possible. With a facial wound this deep, she would have preferred it to have been left to a plastic surgeon—but that wasn't an option out here. All Jaleel had was her, so she would be damned sure she made it as good a job as possible.

By the time she was finished, Jaleel had reluctantly allowed himself to be talked into twelve hours' observation, his colleague had shot off to try to catch up on the mountain of laundry that no doubt awaited her, and the report logged in the computer system, Isla looked up to see Jordanna, Dr Turner and a couple of other medical staff approaching her.

'Nice job, Dr Sinclair.' Jordanna smiled welcomingly.

'Isla,' she corrected instantly, relieved that her first impression had apparently gone down so well.

'Isla,' the nurse echoed happily.

'Yes, very competent,' the senior doctor commended in a cut-glass accent.

She'd assumed he'd been happy enough when he'd left her to it as she'd started cleaning up the wound, but the confirmation was nice all the same.

'And you're also the doctor who stepped in to look after our rather hot-headed crewman yesterday?'

'I just happened to be on scene.' Isla smiled again.

'Well, I'm glad you could change ships and step into our medical team at the last minute. *Hestia's* loss is *Cassiopeia's* gain indeed.'

'Thank you,' Isla replied sincerely. Her fears about being seen as a cuckoo in the previous doctor's nest were appearing unfounded.

At least they were with the medical team. The same wouldn't necessarily be said for Nikhil.

Nikhil.

Isla shut down the unbidden thought and concentrated on her new colleague.

'Welcome to our ship's medical centre, Dr Sinclair,' the older man continued. 'I'm Dr Turner, as I'm sure you've deduced. When appropriate, you can call me Reginald.'

Presumably *appropriate* would be situations like now, when it was just the medical team, or when it was just officers. Nevertheless, Isla decided that the first time she addressed him should also be more official.

'It's lovely to meet you, Dr Turner.' Isla smiled warmly, eying his outstretched hand for a fraction of a moment before shaking it confidently.

Her training had taught her that shaking hands on board was discouraged, but she imagined that Dr Turner was old school and didn't care much for such regulations. It was his way of getting the measure of his colleagues, and Isla felt a punch of triumph when he gave a tacit nod of approval, before turning to one of the other nurses who Isla had yet to meet.

'I'm Lisa,' announced an Australian nurse.

'Gerd.' A German man stepped forward, clearly the senior nurse.

'Shall we all have some tea, and introduce ourselves properly?' Reginald boomed.

'Good idea.' Gerd grinned, and headed out of

the room and into the beautiful, exotic-flower-strewn reception.

It felt as though she'd passed his first subtle test and he was genuinely pleased to have her on board. Though Nikhil's reaction to the news would inevitably be an entirely different matter. It was impossible to ignore the thought any longer, though she commended herself for doing so well up until that point. She hadn't thought of him when she'd been treating Jaleel. She certainly hadn't thought of him when Head Office had called a few hours ago and asked her—though she didn't think she had genuinely had much choice in the matter—to transfer to the *Cassiopeia.*

Liar, whispered a voice inside her head. *He was the first thing you thought when you got that call.*

Isla's heart jolted abruptly. He was bound to be furious. He'd made it abundantly clear that he didn't sleep with colleagues, and that he was only interested in her because she was going to be on board a different ship.

And now, here she was, the new stand-in doctor on the *Queen Cassiopeia.*

Well, he wasn't the only one who had been thrown by the sudden turn of events, she told herself defiantly. She hadn't planned this. Sleeping with the boss certainly hadn't been on her cruise ship to-do list. And if he thought that she was going to be angling for a repeat performance, then she would be more than happy to set him straight.

After Bradley, there was no way she wanted anything complicated with anyone. Even someone who looked like Nikhil, who *kissed* like Nikhil and never mind the rest of his incredible arsenal of skills.

Abruptly, her traitorous body gave a delicious shiver at the memory.

Could it only be this morning that he'd left her bed? It felt like a lifetime ago. She'd gone down to breakfast alone, somewhere between floating on air after their night together and fighting the strangest sense of…what she could only describe as *loss,* when her mobile had rung and she'd looked down to see the Port-Star company name—and she'd just *known.*

Isla pretended that the little celebratory dance that had started in her belly was because she was effectively being upgraded from a two-week tour of the South Americas on the *Jewel of Hestia* to a two-month round-the-world tour on the stunning *Queen Cassiopeia.*

The truth, she feared, was far more shameful. Her body wasn't spinning crazily at the fact that

the cruise liner was the best ship in the fleet—
possibly the world; it was spiralling madly at the
fact that it was *Nikhil's* ship. And some naïve part
of herself appeared to be holding onto the fantasy
notion that, on some secret level, Nikhil might
be a tiny bit pleased to see her too.

'Have you seen around our little terrain down
here?' Reginald asked, hauling her back to the
present.

'Yes, I showed Isla the consultation rooms, the
crew ward and the private rooms for the passengers before the emergency,' Jordanna announced quickly, clearly not wanting to be seen
to be slacking.

'It's more luxurious than any medical centre
I've ever worked in before.' Isla laughed.

'Isn't it?' The senior doctor's proud smile said
it all. 'Not to mention the fact that we get to see
the world. I might not have the private practice
that some of my former med school compatri-
ots might have, but how many of them can inter-
sperse their surgeries with visits to the Pyramids
in Egypt, the Sydney Opera House or the Nor-
wegian fjords?'

'So we do get to visit these places?' Isla asked.

'Yes.'

'Often.'

'It's an amazing lifestyle,' chorused the three nurses simultaneously.

'They said so on the course, and in the training documents,' Isla admitted. 'But I didn't know if it really worked well in practice.'

'It works,' Reginald assured her. 'Normally, at the start of every cruise, our team gets together and calls dibs on the places they really want to visit. Because you're coming in partway through, you've missed out on that, so you'll have to make do with the sights that Dr Morris—the doctor you've replaced—chose, but I'm sure you'll be happy.'

'I can't recall all of his selections,' Gerd added, 'but I think some of them included a banana plantation in Ecuador, a high-speed boating afternoon in Mexico and an exclusive restaurant in Los Angeles. Although I think one of those might have been as a shore doctor on duty.'

'Lucky you.' Lisa laughed. 'Ecuador is coming up soon.'

'I have a museum in Peru and the Panama Canal,' Reginald added. 'So, you see, we keep one doctor on duty onboard, and the other can go ashore.'

'And we usually keep one nurse on board, whilst the other two can go ashore.' Lisa grinned. 'It isn't a bad way to see the world.'

'It isn't bad at all,' agreed Isla.

'Lisa and I are going for a break below; shall we show you around?' Jordanna asked suddenly. 'Surgery isn't for another couple of hours, and Gerd is on duty until then.'

'Sure; that would be lovely.' Isla fought to sound even, and calm.

Being invited to join the two nurses was proof that they had begun to like her, which would make the entire transition a lot easier.

'You don't want to join us?' Lisa grinned at Reginald, who grinned back.

'No, thank you, my dear. Very kind, though.'

Isla recalled some of the trainers on her familiarisation course telling her that the hierarchy on a ship was one of the most important anywhere. It dictated whether you were confined to the hot, smelly bowels of the ship, or whether you got to tread the immaculate hallways of the glamorous passenger decks.

She couldn't imagine Dr Reginald Turner frequenting the crew bars or being part of the bed-hopping culture that she'd been assured existed. Although, given the glint in his eye, she imagined he might have had some fun in his free and single youth.

Well, she might be single but she had no intention of being part of any bed-hopping. Last night with Nikhil was the only action she intended to have for the next few months. As a minimum.

'Did you have your interview with the Captain?' Lisa asked as the three of them began to stroll down the passageways.

'Yes.' As necessarily brief as it had been. 'He seems decent enough.'

'Yeah, he's okay.' Jordanna nodded. 'Generally fair and runs a good ship. But wait until you see his right-hand man.'

As both nurses let out a low, appreciative whistle, Isla didn't know how she kept putting one foot in front of the other. There was no question they were talking about Nikhil.

'That is one seriously hot male specimen.' Jordanna swooned as Lisa nodded vigorously.

'*Seriously* hot.'

'Practically every woman on this ship has thrown themselves at him at some point,' the American continued. 'Crew, staff and passengers.'

Isla tried to bite her tongue. She didn't want to get sucked into the gossip and yet she couldn't seem to stop herself. It was a terrible compulsion—the likes of which she'd never suffered before.

'He's a player then?' she heard herself ask.

'You'd have thought so—' Lisa grimaced '—but the guy never bites.'

'Maybe he does, in secret?' She didn't know what made her say it, but both nurses laughed out loud.

'Not a chance,' scoffed Lisa, turning to her colleague to back her up.

'You can't have secrets on a ship. It's impossible; we all live in each other's pockets. No matter how discreet, someone is always watching.'

'And talking,' Lisa added. 'Fair warning.'

'Heeded.' Isla forced herself to smile, though now her cheeks felt tight with the effort. 'So he has never slept with anyone? Ever?'

'Not on board ship,' Lisa confirmed. 'Though I imagine there have been women. How could there not have been, the way he looks?'

'You'll understand it better when you see him,' Jordanna agreed. 'People like to gossip, of course. And there are always stories of people who know someone, who know someone, who *heard* he'd slept with someone. But in five years on board the same ships as him, I have never known anyone who could actually substantiate it. And, like I said, ship life has no secrets.'

'Plus there are rumours that he once hooked up with a colleague who was leaving the cruising way of life to set up a café in Spain,' added Lisa. 'But as she was leaving, no one knows for sure.'

Jordanna nodded again. 'You can imagine there have been several girls that desperate to get with him over the years they've applied for transfers in the hope that he would then look at them.'

'And has it worked?' Isla couldn't seem to stop herself from asking.

Lisa snorted scornfully. 'No. They were air-heads if they thought it would.'

'Right.' Isla shrugged. It really shouldn't matter to her one iota what kind of a reputation Nikhil Dara had. 'Well, as one of the senior officers, I doubt we'll see much of him anyway.'

'Certainly not enough.' Jordanna pulled a rue-ful face. 'Part of his job includes safety and se-curity so he does come down here now and then to do his rounds, but certainly not enough.'

'We'd all like to see a lot more of him,' quipped Lisa, her insinuating wink driving home her pun. 'If you know what I mean.'

'We know what you mean, Lisa.' Jordanna rolled her eyes good-naturedly. 'The whole of Chile probably knows what you mean.'

'Says the girl who threw herself on him the first night she was ever on board.'

Isla watched, intrigued, as the stunning American flushed slightly.

'Yes, well, he turned me down without even blinking an eye.'

'The only guy who ever has.' Lisa threaded her arm through her friend's in solidarity, before turning to Isla. 'Makes me feel better about the fact that he's never looked twice at me either, though. If he can turn down Miss USA here, then what chance do the rest of us stand? Although you're pretty striking too, Isla. You both make me feel dowdy by comparison.'

'You're beautiful,' Isla and Jordanna chorused instantly, and both nurses turned to look at her approvingly.

'Yeah—' Lisa grinned '—you'll do fine, Doc. Hard worker, knows her medical stuff and nice to boot. We'll definitely keep you over your condescending predecessor any day.'

'Thanks—' she laughed '—I think.'

And though she didn't mention it, she quietly filed away the fact that the previous doctor apparently hadn't been a good fit for the medical team, and they were glad to have her on board. Somehow, that made the idea of having to face Nikhil that much easier.

Although, with any luck, she wouldn't have to.

The smells and sounds of the crew bar reached

Isla's senses long before they reached the room itself. Even so, she wasn't prepared for the sights as she rounded the corner and stepped through the doors.

It felt as if there were hundreds of crew in the place already mingling with raucous laughter, although it couldn't even be half of those crew on board. And the place was gargantuan. There were TV screens and arcade games, a bank of computers on one wall and a bowling alley on the other. There were even several pool tables, ice-hockey tables and football tables in there. And still there would be room for more.

'Come on.' Jordanna grabbed her hand as the three of them weaved through the people to the bar. 'It's a bit of a shock to the senses, I know, but Lisa will get the drinks, we'll get the seats and you'll soon start to settle.'

Obediently, Isla followed, circling the room twice before Jordanna spotted a small group getting ready to leave a table and pounced.

'Impressive,' Isla commented.

'Yeah, well, in here you have to be faster than a passenger grabbing the last chocolate éclair off the dessert buffet.'

Isla didn't bother to say that passenger would probably have been her mother.

'So this is your first cruise?' Jordanna asked as they shuffled into the seats.

'Yes, I was supposed to be joining the *Jewel of Hestia* tomorrow but...'

'Thank God you're with us,' Jordanna cut in. 'Do a good job and you could probably put in a request to stay here permanently. If you carry on the way you're going, the rest of us would definitely stand character for you. And Reginald holds a lot of sway.'

'The previous doctor was that bad?'

'Worse.' The nurse squeezed her eyes shut as she shook her head. 'Not with the passengers, of course. He was the epitome of a caring doctor to them. But with the crew, and with us...? No, he was horrid.'

For a moment, Isla hesitated. She was desperate to hear more, but starting the job bad-mouthing a colleague who she'd never met wasn't her style. Instead, she opted to change the conversation.

'So what are the patients like?'

That easily, the conversation flipped to medical scenarios, both the routine and the unusual, and when Lisa made her way over with their drinks they indulged in the inexorable horror scenarios.

It was perhaps a good half hour of free-flowing

conversation before the two nurses abruptly fell quiet, leaving Isla to look up from the straw of her drink and see a disapproving Nikhil looming over their table.

'Dr Sinclair, drinking already?'

Isla flashed hot then cold, shock and unwanted excitement coursing through her like petrol, and with the sheer unfairness of his accusation as the match.

She drew in a deep, furious breath. 'I don't think...'

'I'm not asking what you think, Doctor.' He cut her off instantly. 'A word, please. Now.'

CHAPTER SIX

NIKHIL BARELY WAITED for Isla to join him before striding out of the bar and back along the corridor to the bank of crew-only elevators, trying not to think about where they'd been heading the last time they'd been in an elevator together.

And wasn't that the problem?

Seeing her sitting there in the bar, already so at home with his crew, was like a punch to the gut. Not least because he'd been *glad* to see her there.

What the hell was that about?

He never liked to mix professional and private. Yet, in that moment, the only thing he'd really wanted to do was get her alone and pick back up where they'd left off that morning.

He simply hadn't been able to help himself from heading over to her. The woman was like some kind of opiate, and he seemed hell-bent on getting a high. If he'd walked away, no one would have known any different. Instead, he'd marched up to her in front of half of the rest of the medical staff and made some kind of damned scene.

All because he wanted Isla Sinclair, with a ferocity that he'd never experienced before.

Stepping inside the elevator beside him, she turned around and folded her arms over her chest, a hint of mulishness about her delicious mouth.

'I didn't ask for this transfer,' she announced.

'Not here, please,' he clipped out swiftly.

'You think someone's going to overhear us?'

'Not here,' he repeated simply. A command, not a request.

And possibly more to keep his own charging, roaring emotions in check than anything else. Still, Nikhil wouldn't have been surprised if she'd made a point of non-compliance. But, even though she exhaled deeply, she didn't try to say anything more, and Nikhil was left to his own thoughts.

The overriding one being that he should feel more aggrieved than he did that she was here, on *his* ship.

He'd received the call from Head Office a few hours ago informing him that, to expedite handovers, they'd opted to transfer a Dr Sinclair to his ship because she happened to be in Chile.

She might never have told him her surname,

but his gut had known instantly it was her. If he hadn't been caught up with a safety boat issue on the crew decks he probably would have been the one to conduct her interview in place of the Captain.

He was glad he hadn't. It had taken all this time for him to get his head straight. If he even had it straight now.

Deep in the logical side of his brain he knew it made sense. She was in Chile waiting for the *Hestia* to arrive, once the *Cassiopeia* had left. So assigning her to this ship meant that they wouldn't be late leaving port. Apparently, another doctor who was, even now, airborne and on their way to this port would be better placed to join the *Hestia* instead.

But it wasn't the efficacy of the transfer that concerned him the most. This thing that was worming its way through him wasn't annoyance or aggravation. It was something far, far more dangerous. More inappropriate.

It was altogether too much like *pleasure*. A sort of *thrill* that she was here—on *his* ship. And as much as Nikhil tried to punch it down, it wouldn't go.

He, who had spent his entire career zealously avoiding blurring the lines between his personal life and his professional one.

He'd known he had a problem last night when they'd had sex—maybe even before that. He'd wanted it—*her*—too much. With a ferocity that he couldn't explain. And when he'd left that morning it had taken all he'd had not to turn around and stay, just that little bit longer.

And longer, again.

So what did it say that the urge to pull her into his arms, right here and now, and take up where they'd left off that morning was so damned strong?

He clenched his fists tightly and thrust them into the pockets of his uniform. He could smell the light hint of coconut in her shampoo from here, pervading his nostrils and conjuring up images he was a desperately trying not to see, his mind echoing with memories of her gasps and cries as he'd licked her to ecstasy.

What would she do if, right now, he pressed her against that wall, slid his fingers into her waistband and indulged in all that soft, wet heat that was, even now, making him hard, aching, in a way that no one else had ever made him feel?

God, how he wanted to.

Clenching his jaw until it was locked so tight that it was actually painful, Nikhil glowered at some abstract point on the metal doors in front of him. He was grateful when the elevator drew to a halt and the doors finally opened, finally releasing him from the temptations of that enclosed space.

Marching down the corridor to his office, he didn't even stop to see if Isla was following. Opening the door, he held it open and wordlessly ushered her inside.

'Like I said,' she began, even before the door had closed behind them or he'd made his way around the other side—the safe side—of his desk, 'I didn't ask for this transfer, but what was I supposed to say when they contacted me? *No, sorry, I can't. I just slept with the ship's First Officer, and he won't like it?*'

'So you did realise that I wouldn't welcome your arrival?' he managed curtly, wondering why the words that were coming out of his mouth sounded so awkward. So hollow.

'No, actually, I didn't consider you at all.'

She met his eyes for a brief moment, then let them slide away. She was lying; they both knew it. Although why it should make him feel so victorious was a different matter.

'Then now is the time to start.'

'I'm not quitting.' Her head snapped up in an instant.

'I'm not asking you to. I'm well aware it was a Head Office decision.'

'Really? Because you're acting like I'm at least partly to blame.' She sighed, raking her hand through her hair.

He remembered too clearly how soft it felt. That vaguely coconut scent. His traitorous body twitched in response, but he quashed it furiously.

Then...what?

'We can't change what happened,' he said grimly, making himself sit down behind the desk, and gesturing for Isla to do the same. 'But I want to establish the rules from here on in.'

For himself, as much as for her. Since the sight of her standing there, her uniform lovingly fitting her curves—too pristine and perfect—was making him think of all kinds of ways to sully it.

He felt like some sex-crazed kid. Worse, he kind of liked this new sensation.

'I told you that I don't do relationships.' He wasn't sure if he was reminding Isla or himself. He'd never had to remind himself of anything like that before.

'So I hear.' Her eyes narrowed at him, too sharply for Nikhil's liking. 'You like to keep yourself single and available.'

It was about as far from the truth as it was possible to get. And yet, as reasons went, why not go with it? It would be more likely to put her off than anything else, and Lord knew he needed help to stay away from this woman.

There had been no reason for him to speak to her at all, and yet he'd found himself in that bar, having sought her out.

For what, exactly?

'I never promised you exclusivity, Isla,' he bit out, though every word tasted bitter in his mouth.

Did they sound as hollow as they felt?

'No. And I don't recall asking for it, now,' she pointed out evenly.

He might have expected her to appear more manipulative. They usually were, which was why he generally liked to be able to walk away. Only right now he seemed to be the one having the most trouble with that concept. If he'd been a lesser man it might have dented his ego.

What the hell was wrong with him?

'You think you're the only one? That you're somehow special? That we're going to pick up where we left off now we're working on the same ship together?'

He'd intended the words to score a hit, but when she blanched he actually felt it like a physical blow. He opened his mouth to apologise, but something stopped him.

Wasn't this what he'd intended? Still, he waited,

needing to hear whatever it was she was going to say.

'I understand that your one-night stand suddenly being transferred to your ship is a shock.' Isla eyed him contemptuously. 'But trust me, I'm no less thrown by it than you are.'

'Good, so long as you don't have…expectations of us now embarking on some great love affair.'

He was acting like a jerk. It was so unlike him, and yet he couldn't seem to get a grip. Yet another example of how she made him feel like some untried kid.

'I told you, this is a fresh start for me. I certainly don't need to get tangled up with any jackass men,' she added pointedly. 'Talking of love, which never really exists.'

Something he couldn't identify, or didn't want to, caught at him. Whether she'd intended it or not, he found himself hooked, reeled in—wanting to know more. Keen to uncover whatever her opinion of *love* was, in the puzzle that was Dr Isla Sinclair.

But he hadn't brought her here to piece her together in his head. He'd come here to remind them both that there could be no repeat of what had happened between them in Chile.

Only the previous night?

It felt like a lifetime ago—could it really have been that recent? Could it only have been hours ago that they had shared a bed? That he'd held her body against his, and around him?

Despite all his brain's objections, something slammed inside his chest. He might have thought it was his heart picking up pace, if he'd actually *had* a heart. If it hadn't been killed years ago, when he'd plunged that knife into his raging father.

And still he couldn't remember it. Guilt had blocked it out too tightly, clearly. Even now, trying to push that guilt down, Nikhil found himself scrabbling for something else to hold onto. A distraction that would grant him a desperate reprieve.

'Why are we here, Nikhil?' she demanded suddenly. 'Why do we need to clarify anything? Why not just stay away from each other?'

'I'm First Officer on this ship and you—thanks to Head Office's little shuffles—are now my junior doctor. Our working paths will unquestionably cross. Regularly. I've worked hard at my career, and at keeping my private life wholly removed from my professional one.'

'And what?' she snapped, and he found it fascinating the way her eyes sparked when she was angry. He suspected very few people ever got to see this side of the unflappable Dr Sinclair. 'You think I'm here to broadcast our liaison to the entire ship?'

'Some women in your position might.'

She snorted—actually *snorted*—at him. He wasn't sure anyone had ever snorted at him— at least, not in the last decade. It was so…unexpected.

'It might have escaped your notice, in your essentially Nikhil-centric way of thinking, but that's *my* private life that would be on show too. And I value my career as much as you do. Possibly more, given that, despite all the advances we women have made, who I sleep with will come under more scrutiny than who *you* sleep with.'

'I can't say that I remember much sleeping going on,' he quipped, before he could stop himself.

Suddenly, in spite of everything, he found himself grinning at her little cry of frustration. She got under his skin that easily.

'My God, you're unreasonable.'

He didn't realise when he'd moved, or how he came to be standing in front of her, but suddenly he was there, within touching distance of her. That dark thing inside him railing in its cage, howling for things it had no right to crave.

'On the contrary,' he grated out. 'I am the epitome of reason.'

At least he usually was. Before this woman had come along and turned everything upside down.

He took another step closer.

'What are you doing, Nikhil?' Isla asked.

But her voice had changed. Breathy, and fragile, and hesitant, and she watched him with that expression that made him hard and melting all at once.

It was impossible. *She* was impossible. And yet she was right…*here.*

'I don't know what you want from me,' she said, her voice thick, echoing every emotion swirling through his own body.

'You know precisely what I want.' There had to be some kind of remedy for this madness he felt every time she was in the room. But if there was, he feared that right now he wouldn't even take it.

'Because I want it too,' he heard himself growl.

She stirred him up in a way that no other woman had ever done, electrifying him and challenging him in equal measure.

She swallowed. Hard. And her bashfulness was all the more bewitching.

'I…don't know anything of the sort.'

'Then it appears I have no choice but to employ the only means to show you, *pyar*,' he growled.

And then, as if he couldn't make it any worse, he bent his head and kissed her.

Isla felt as though she was falling. Fast, and hard, with no idea what was at the bottom. And she couldn't seem to bring herself to care.

She tried to cling to some last grain of reality, but it was slipping further away with every foot that she fell.

And she was plummeting.

How was it that this kiss was so different from any last night, when she thought that they'd spent the entire night kissing. And touching. And tasting. Yet this was something different again. More intense, somehow. As though neither of them wanted to give into temptation, and at the same time as if there was nowhere else either of them wanted to be.

She knew it was wrong—certainly on an intellectual level. Hadn't they just been asserting— vociferously—their respective career choices? Hadn't they both just agreed that private lives and professional lives were clear and distinct entities which had no business becoming complicated?

And yet here they were, complicating things

in the most base, primal way possible. And as wrong as Isla knew it was, she couldn't stop herself from wanting more.

Much more.

It was possibly the most thrilling, terrifying sensation that she had ever experienced. A complete loss of control, and a complete inability to care.

So long as Nikhil never stopped kissing her.

Isla was aware of nothing. And everything. Like his tongue gliding over her lips, parting them so effortlessly, and dipping so wickedly inside. Like his large hand, splayed against her back and holding her close, so deliciously close, to him. Like the way every inch of her body moulded itself, as if instinctively, to every inch of his.

It was like fire. More than that—an inferno, and she was dancing in the flames.

With every twist of his mouth against hers, and every tangle of his tongue, she made a tiny new sound in her throat. Greedy, eager, impatient. She hungered for him more than she'd hungered for anything. Even her job on this ship, it seemed.

But, rather than helping her to stop, the knowledge only made her feel that much more desperate. More daring. He made her feel glorious and proud, as if she could do anything. Even walk on the very water that encircled this ship.

If this was him keeping away from her, then she couldn't say she was complaining. Though some part of her whispered that she should.

And then his hands were moving over her. Leisurely, lazy, yet still they scorched a path as they went, leaving her quivering with heat, and fresh need. Tracing the contours of her sides and the dip of her back he slowly—too slowly—began to pull her shirt out of her trousers.

She shivered with anticipation, and damn him if the devilish man didn't smile. She could feel the curve of his mouth against her throat, kissing her in that oh-so-sensitive hollow below her ear.

'Nikhil...' His name escaped her mouth before she could stop it.

But, if anything, it only made him haul her to him even tighter. As if the sound of his name on her lips drove him on all the more.

Sliding his hands beneath the fabric, he traced a series of whorls higher—even higher—making her breath catch in her throat in her restlessness.

'Patience, *pyar*,' he told her.

But she didn't miss the tautness in his voice— all the evidence she needed that he barely held onto his own patience. She couldn't help it; she rolled her hips against him—then exulted when they both groaned softly.

And then, as he held her waist with one hand, he finally allowed the other to reach higher, nudging her breast aside and raking one thumb pad over her straining nipple.

Isla arched instinctively against him. She heard the low cry, but it took a moment to realise it was herself.

'I've missed these.' Nikhil's voice rumbled through her, as dark as the inky ocean, and just as deep.

As though it hadn't only been this morning that he'd left her bed.

As though it had been a whole eternity.

Part of her felt as though it must surely have been that long. And she didn't understand how, though her mind had replayed last night several times already—in spectacular detail—it had somehow failed to recapture quite the intensity of the effect Nikhil had on her.

Her mind had somehow played it down. That didn't seem possible. But it wasn't playing it down now; it was sending her wild and flooding her with a sense of lust that she could hardly believe she'd denied existed only twenty-four hours before.

Before she'd met Nikhil.

Now, she could do nothing but give into that fervour. More than that, she was practically racing towards it.

It was ludicrous the way her body reacted with memories and anticipation, and all she could do was press herself against him—hot steel against her softest part. Full of promise.

It was a noise outside the cabin door that finally broke into their fragile, fictitious little bubble. The voices of crew who could only be officers, talking confidently outside the room—reminding Isla and Nikhil exactly where they were. And what they were supposed to be doing.

Or perhaps, more the point, what they weren't supposed to be doing.

In one smooth movement, Nikhil swung her away from him and set her down, turning to stalk back to his desk whilst Isla scrambled to get her head together. And her clothing straight.

'This was a mistake.'

His words lashed through the air, and she was almost surprised when they didn't physically cut into her flesh.

'How very clichéd of you.' She barely recognised her own voice in her effort not to fold under his glower. 'Disappointingly so, in fact.'

'Is everything a joke to you, Dr Sinclair?'

'Dr Sinclair?' She was proud that her voice

didn't waver too badly. 'Do you think that addressing each other formally can erase what just happened between us?'

'Clearly, we need some boundaries.'

'Boundaries?' She narrowed her eyes at him.

'I warned you that nothing more could happen between us again. And yet here we are.'

Isla busied herself tucking her shirt in, not quite trusting herself to answer straight away.

How had it come to this? She'd been so careful all her life, and then last night she'd met Nikhil and she'd decided that one night—just for once—she could throw caution to the wind.

And now she was standing in her boss's office—technically her boss's boss's office—her clothes in disarray, a low, molten ache deep within and her legs threatening to buckle beneath her at any moment. And now Nikhil seemed to be laying it all at her feet.

It was too much to bear.

'You say it like you think this is entirely *my* fault,' she managed at last. Then lifted her eyes to his with as much defiance as she could muster. 'Or have I misunderstood?'

He'd called her *pyar.*

My love.

Nikhil glowered across the room, torn between

contemplating the madness of having sent her away from him just now and the lunacy of having brought her to his office in the first instance.

He had no idea how he'd managed to tear himself away from her. He had even less idea how he managed to stand in place, around the other side of the desk from her, as though it could provide some barrier between them.

As though it made her any less of a siren, and him any less the mariner drawn inexorably to her.

Although that would suggest that he was powerless and she was deliberately luring him, when the truth was that they were equal victims to this all-consuming attraction that crackled between them.

Not that his current state of fury at himself would allow him to admit that much aloud.

'You're a distraction, Isla,' he ground out instead. 'And I don't do *distractions*.'

He knew the moment he spoke the words that they were a mistake. They revealed far too many things that he would much rather have kept to himself.

He watched as Isla's eyes widened then crinkled, seeing his unexpected weakness for herself.

It was galling.

'Is that so?' She arched her eyebrows. 'How

flattering that I'm a distraction. I wouldn't have thought that the savagely determined Nikhil Dara would have allowed anything to sway him.'

'I didn't say that I intended to allow anything to *sway* me,' he bit back.

'And yet here we are. With you taking time to drag me to your office just to kiss me and then tell me…what? That you don't intend to waste time being distracted by me?'

She had a point, but that wasn't the worst of it. No, the worst of it was that he—who had prided himself on control and restraint all these years—was now fighting the considerable urge to silence her with his mouth—*again*—whilst he stripped them both and worshipped her body the way he'd been dreaming about doing since he'd walked away from her hotel room.

It certainly didn't help that she wanted him every bit as badly. He knew women well enough to see it in the lines of her body. He could read it in every dark flash of her eyes, every deep breath she inhaled, every time she flicked her tongue out over her lips.

And every single one of her reactions only served to stoke that fire even higher, making it burn hotter and brighter until he feared his entire body might burst into flame.

It was ludicrous.

They'd had sex, just as he'd had sex with women before. Not an obscene amount of women—not like some of the officers he knew, who seemed incapable of preventing their trousers from ruling their heads, on practically a daily basis—but still, he didn't do repeat performances. It wasn't worth the hassle.

Which only made it all the more infuriating that he couldn't seem to shake this woman from his head. He wanted her.

His body *needed* her. And that simply wouldn't do.

He would stay away from Dr Isla Sinclair if it killed him.

CHAPTER SEVEN

THE BANANA PLANTATION was vast and dense, bustling with people. Isla followed the local tour guide with fascination, watching as men chopped down enormous clusters of bananas, already wrapped in plastic bagging.

'Did you know it isn't really a banana tree but a banana plant?'

She turned slowly to face Nikhil, her heart hammering so loudly in her chest that it was surely impossible that he couldn't hear it.

One moment she'd been rather enjoying her tour of one of Ecuador's—and apparently the world's—biggest producer of organic bananas, learning about hands and fingers and tiers, and watching as the workers loaded enormous bagged bunches onto a rail system, and the next she found herself face to face with the person she'd been trying so hard to shove out of her head.

It had been almost a week since their encounter in Nikhil's office, and she'd been congratulating herself on having managed to keep her distance from him.

Or at least she'd told herself that she *ought* to be congratulating herself.

She'd told herself that she didn't feel anything remotely akin to regret that things had turned out the way they had. Turning something that had been so electrifying and fun that night in Chile into something infinitely uglier. And sombre.

With such thoughts whirling around her brain, Isla wasn't sure how she managed to tug her expression into something she hoped was a light, airy expression.

'Mr Dara, what a surprise. I thought we were keeping our distance from each other. Or, more accurately, that I was to keep my distance from *you*.' Her voice sounded remarkably even. 'According to you, I'm too much of a distraction.'

She had no idea how she managed to infuse her words with condemnation, but she found she was rather proud of herself. Still, if she could have bound her erratic heart down with ropes and chains, she would have done.

'You are a distraction,' he replied easily. 'How else do you explain the fact that, instead of concentrating on the tour, I'm talking to you?'

'Perhaps you have a childlike attention span?' she quipped. 'I've inherited all the tours and duties of the doctor who I've replaced, and I'm here as the medical liaison in the event of any accident. Why are you here?'

'So you had no choice in this day-trip?'

'None at all. I'm sorry if it bruises your evidently swollen ego.' She made sure not to sound remotely sorry.

It was galling, but he didn't bite as she'd anticipated. Instead, something she might have taken to be amusement—had she not already known that Nikhil didn't have an amused bone in his body—tugged at his lips.

'No doubt I can get my fragile ego massaged back into shape, if need be,' he drawled.

Isla batted away a sharp stab of some emotion that she told herself couldn't possibly have been jealousy.

'No doubt you can,' she muttered darkly. 'Though you might watch what you pick up. I've just had to treat a rather nasty outbreak of genital warts and gonorrhoea that's ripping through a good proportion of the crew.'

'I'm aware, since all your reports ultimately come to me. But thank you for your concern.'

'It isn't concern.' Isla narrowed her eyes.

'Really? It sounded like concern.'

'Well, it wasn't.'

So much for trying to rile him; he was enjoying

this far too much. But didn't that beg the question, *Why was she trying so hard to rile him?*

'I also happen to know that you've treated two heart attacks, a sprained ankle, a honeymooner's unexpected pregnancy and multiple passengers with known allergies who happened to decide that the food in question looked just that bit too tempting to pass up. And that's just amongst the passengers.'

'Right... Well, then... I guess that's you up to speed.'

Isla faltered, not sure what to say next, or even where to go. But then a shriek from the main excursion party a hundred metres or so ahead drew everyone's attention as Isla and Nikhil raced to the passenger.

'I've been bitten, I've been bitten...' The man was already beginning to panic. 'Is it a spider? I think I killed it, but it's still in my shirt. Get it out. You've got to get it out.'

As Isla began dealing with the man, a couple of the locals came running over. There was no obvious sign of a bite but, sure enough, in the man's shirt was a dead spider. As the two plantation workers peered at it, the passenger began to hyperventilate.

'Oh, God, I'm going to die out here.'

'No.' One of the workers lifted his head with a smile. 'Is not problem. Not bad spider.'

'Irritado,' the other added, making an itching action with his hands. *'No es venenoso.'*

A collective sigh went around the group. Most of them were clearly relieved, but a couple looked a little disappointed not to be treated to a more exciting show. Isla wasn't surprised when Nikhil took charge, reclaiming all the passengers' attention and getting the tour back on track as their guide moved them a little further from the action.

Isla crouched down carefully by her patient.

'Are you known to be allergic, Mr…?'

'Camberwell.' He didn't look convinced. 'You're sure it isn't venomous? I feel sick. I think I'm going to die.'

'Can we get him to shelter?' Isla asked as Nikhil materialised by her side. 'And maybe a chair, and some ice?'

He barely seemed to lift his hand before a couple of plantation workers hurried over, listening intently as he rattled off a few commands to them in Spanish. Firm, yet not imperious— *typically Nikhil*, as she was beginning to understand.

'Sí, sí.' The men made a chair with their hands and proceeded to carry the still overwrought Mr

Camberwell from the plantation area to the processing plant.

Isla and Nikhil followed quickly.

'I still want him checked over properly,' Nikhil murmured.

'Of course,' she confirmed as the workers settled her patient onto a rickety chair.

She shot them a smile. *'Gracias.'*

'De nada.'

She turned her focus to her patient, not surprised when Nikhil launched into his own conversation with the men. But Mr Camberwell was her priority. She swung her little daysack off her bag, complete with some emergency medical supplies.

'All right, sir, let's check you over. I'm just going to take your pulse.'

Methodically, Isla checked her patient's pulse, breathing and reactions, applying an ice pack as soon as it arrived from the workers.

His blood pressure seemed fine, and the initial shock of the bite seemed to be wearing off now. Carefully she lifted the ice pack up and checked the area. There was perhaps the beginning of a little redness and swelling.

'It itches,' Mr Camberwell grumbled, trying to push her hand away to scratch it.

'Of course, sir—' Isla flashed her best smile

'—but try not to scratch it, as that can make it worse. I'm going to clean it out for you now and apply a little antibiotic ointment, and then I think it's best to get you back to the ship and to the medical bay, just to check you over again.'

'Yes, yes.' Mr Camberwell nodded enthusiastically.

'Okay, so in the meantime I'm also going to give you an antihistamine to help with the itching.'

She began to quickly clean the area to prevent infection, keeping the man talking as she did so, more and more confident that it wasn't going to develop into something any more serious. Finally, she stood up and drew Nikhil to one side.

'Shall I return to the ship with Mr Camberwell?'

'What's the probability that his situation is going to develop?'

Isla wrinkled her nose. 'I can't say with absolute certainty, of course, but I'm confident that it's just a bite that's going to hurt and itch for a few days. I'd still like him kept under observation in the medical centre for twenty-four hours.'

'So you're better staying with this tour group, in the event of any other emergency,' Nikhil confirmed.

Isla nodded. 'Agreed, although Mr Camberwell should have someone to accompany him back to the ship.'

'Understood.'

Turning back to the party, Nikhil beckoned one of the shore excursion staff, who seemed only too eager to race over to him, her doe eyes growing wider as Nikhil began to instruct her.

One could only hope that she herself didn't look so besotted when talking to Nikhil, Isla thought irritably as she concentrated on the understandably still concerned Mr Camberwell. Not helped by the unwelcome thrill that she'd felt when she'd realised she would still get to spend another couple of hours of this excursion with Nikhil.

What was wrong with her that she couldn't push him into her past, the way he seemed to have done so easily with her? Was his appeal so great?

It had to be. Even now, she couldn't stop herself from admiring the way he was so effortlessly able to take control in any given situation. Calming yet authoritative.

And almost universally adored, of course. Men and women, passengers and crew. *That* certainly helped his appeal—and none of *them* had slept with him.

So what chance did *she* stand?

Especially when she couldn't shake the thought that, for all his words about never crossing that line between personal and professional, when he talked to her there was still an intensity in those dark, expressive eyes that she'd never, *ever* seen when he talked to anyone else.

Whatever Nikhil said, he hadn't quite pushed her into his past the way he would have her—and maybe even himself—believe.

Perhaps for him it was more about the physical, more about the sexual desire. Maybe he hadn't got quite that same kick of pleasure at the realisation that they would be spending the afternoon in each other's company. But neither was he entirely indifferent—and didn't they say that *indifference* was worse than anything?

Shaking her thoughts free, Isla busied herself tending to her patient and making a few notes, but it was no use. Her mind was filling with a slew of memories from that night. So vivid, and so real. That powerful body pressed against hers, making her *feel* things she'd never felt before. Her body shivered from the sheer memory of it, despite the heat.

'Right Mr Camberwell, let's get you back to the ship, shall we?' Nikhil's voice pierced her thoughts. Bright and firm enough to instil confidence into her worried patient, who looked up instantly, his watery eyes clearing as he took Nikhil's outstretched arm and allowed himself to be helped to his feet. Gathering up the last of her kit, Isla hurried after them as they headed for the vehicle.

A few more instructions, and the Jeep was heading off down the plantation path. But when Isla made herself turn around she realised the main excursion party had disappeared, around to some different area of the tightly packed banana stems. Now, she was alone with Nikhil, save for the processing staff who were all too busy concentrating on their production line to pay the two of them any attention.

'Well done,' he said quietly, turning to face her.

The full force of his gaze sent a primitive wave of heat crashing through her.

Isla forced herself to laugh. 'What for? Doing my job?'

'Doing it so quietly that none of the other guests have felt panicked enough to return to the ship along with Mr Camberwell. It happens,' he added when she frowned in surprise.

'Oh.'

It was all she could think of. Her mind had gone blank.

'You are always so discreet, Isla. It's a surprising quality, particularly on a cruise ship like ours, I find.'

The compliment was as unexpected as it was sincere, catching Isla off-guard. For a moment she flailed around for a response.

'Careful, Nikhil.' She swallowed at last. 'That almost sounded like a compliment.'

'Perhaps because it *was* a compliment. Though I'm glad to hear you've dispensed with the Mr Dara nonsense.'

Isla opened her mouth to object, but a gurgle of laughter came bubbling out instead. Unintended but, it turned out, the perfect way to break the tension.

'I could have called you *sir*; you are the First Officer, after all.'

He let out a low, deep chuckle of his own and before she could stop herself she seized it, filing it away somewhere special like the dragon hoarding its treasure. Or the chimera hiding the lost Inca gold, that Reginald had been telling them all about after his return from his day-trip to Peru.

'You wouldn't call me *sir* even if you had to,' he noted. Accurately, as it turned out.

'Not even if you commanded me,' she agreed.

But she wasn't prepared for the way his eyes suddenly grew hot. Hungry. Reflecting all the things she was trying to keep stuffed down, so deep inside.

'And what commands would you obey, Isla? If I uttered them?'

'None,' she retorted.

But her voice was hoarser than normal. A fact of which they were both aware.

She had no intention of adding any more, but then her mouth started talking all of its own accord.

'And what about you, Nikhil? What commands would you obey if *I* issued them?'

He took a step closer to her, and the whole world suddenly receded until it was just her and Nikhil. No one else existed for Isla. Not the plantation, not the workers, not even the tour group, only just out of sight around that corner.

'Do you really want to know?'

His tone was so heavy, so loaded, that it fired straight through Isla, pooling between her legs. Making her molten in an instant.

'Yes.' But it was barely more than a whisper.

It was odd, the way everything seemed so loud and yet so still. She could hear monkeys calling to each other, birds singing the most wondrous songs and insects chirping and squeaking. Yet at the same time she didn't think she could hear anything above the roaring in her ears.

She had no idea how long they stood there, staring at each other, some invisible thread binding them together, tighter and tighter, until she couldn't move.

Or didn't want to.

And still he didn't answer. He didn't speak at all. Yet she could hear his thoughts swirling through her. All the things he wanted to do to her, right there. All the things she wanted too.

Just when she'd begun to think he was never going to speak, he opened his mouth and murmured the words, only loud enough for her to hear.

'Why don't you try it and find out?'

And Isla didn't think twice. She lifted herself up onto her tiptoes, in her heavy, leather walking boots, and she kissed him, the way she'd been dreaming of doing all week.

And then he was kissing her. His lips slipping smoothly over hers, his tongue moving languorously as he tasted her, sampled her. Over and over again.

Unhurried and unfettered, as if they had hours. Days. Perhaps whole lifetimes. Another level again from the passion of that night they'd spent together, and somehow that made her tremble all the more.

His fingers traced her jaw, leaving her skin scorched in their wake. He made her feel infinitely precious, and utterly desired. No other man had ever made her feel so...*aware.* Aware of him. And aware of herself.

That night, he'd awakened something in her that she hadn't even known had been lying dormant. She'd told herself that she'd been in complete control of the passion of that night. She'd chosen to pursue the novelty of a one-night encounter with the clichéd tall, dark stranger, leading to her first ever one-night stand. At thirty-two, she'd decided to lose herself in a way she'd never done before.

But now, here, alone with Nikhil, she was finally forced to concede the truth. She hadn't been in control at all. It hadn't been about that night, or that place. It had been about *him.* Nikhil. She doubted any other tall, dark or handsome stranger would have made her lose herself the way that he had done. *He* made her feel things she'd never felt before. *He* made her discover more about herself. And the worst of it was that she wanted to learn more.

This was insanity, Nikhil thought as he knocked on the door to Isla's cabin.

He didn't realise he'd been holding his breath until she opened the door. And stared at him.

'Nikhil?'

'Can I come in? I'd rather not stand here in the hallway outside your room for longer than necessary.'

Her eyes gleamed at him then narrowed, echoes of their last encounter practically bouncing off the walls around them. And even though her stance was defiant, her voice was careful and low. Discreet.

'If you've come to insult me again, like the other day, then I'd rather you didn't. I don't need you to come here to tell me that you regret kissing me earlier, and I'd rather you dealt with your guilt yourself. Quietly. In your own room.'

He didn't answer. Didn't tell her that the only thing he regretted was the fact that they'd had to stop, before the tour group walked back around the corner and spotted them. Or that he regretted that the excursion was so long that he'd been forced to carry on with the afternoon as though he was enjoying himself, when the only thing he'd wanted to do was get back here—and come right here, to her room.

But Nikhil didn't say any of that. It was hard enough to admit it to himself, without having to admit it to someone else. Even Isla.

Especially Isla.

'Can I come in?' he repeated simply.

She glowered at him a moment longer before sighing heavily. 'Apparently, I don't have a choice.'

He didn't answer. He merely followed her inside and closed the door.

'Why are you here, Nikhil?' she demanded, when he didn't speak. But he didn't miss the slight quake in her voice. 'To tell me that you regret what happened at the plantation? Because you've already made it clear we should stay away from each other, not give into distractions.'

And still he didn't answer. He had no idea what he *was* doing there, only that his legs seemed to have carried him along the corridors to her room, all of their own accord. The only thing he knew was that a week ago he'd sworn he'd stay away from this woman if it killed him.

He thought it damned near had.

How many times had he thought he'd seen her retreating around a corner just as he'd arrived? Or imagined he could smell that soft, lightly floral scent in the air as he walked down a corridor?

How many times had he found a reason to be near the medical centre when he could arguably have left it to another officer?

'Look, Nikhil—' she twisted her hands in midair in front of him '—I made a mistake earlier, and I'm sorry. I wouldn't want to distract you and mess up your head. Or your career. Or whatever.'

'It's already messed up,' he heard himself say, though he didn't clarify what, precisely, felt messed up.

Perhaps because he wasn't sure he knew the answer to that either. He only knew that, oddly, it felt like a good messed-up. As if he was messed up with Isla. How was it that the only time he ever really felt like himself—like the real Nikhil—was when he was with her?

It should be exactly the opposite. She made him act crazily, when he was all about control. How was that the *real him*?

He let out a low sound, not wanting to think about that right now. He just had to fight this impossibly overwhelming urge to put his hands on her shoulders and haul her to him, to claim that pink, perfect mouth with his, just like he had a lifetime ago.

He seemed to have no control where Isla Sinclair was concerned, and yet suddenly he couldn't bring himself to care. The rules he'd made for himself—rules that had worked flawlessly all these years—had been in disarray ever since she'd walked onto his ship.

Or even before that, when he'd been called to that damned bar brawl.

This wasn't how things were meant to be. His career wasn't supposed to merge with his personal life. It couldn't. Because each needed to be kept in its own box—one that he could pick up easily when it was time and put down just as easily when he needed to. But Isla didn't fit that black and white mould.

She didn't fit *any* mould.

She was too fluid, and vibrant, and...challenging. She was upturning all those carefully ordered boxes, spilling the contents of his life out onto the floor and mixing them up. And, for all his statements about not blurring the lines, he wasn't really preventing her.

Worse, he was *encouraging* her. *He* was the one who had kissed her back at the banana plantation, and *he* was the one who had come to her cabin now.

'I came to apologise,' he lied. Because that hadn't been in the forefront of his mind when he'd stalked the corridors to get here—though it should have been.

'To apologise?' Her eyebrows shot up, as if she didn't believe him either.

She already knew him too well, and what did it say that he liked the idea of that?

'You're right.' He dipped his head. 'It *was* me who called you a distraction, but kissed you today. It *is* me who is seeking you out now, to try to make things…less fraught between us. To make sure that, after this afternoon, I haven't given you false hope.'

'False hope?' she echoed again, this time in disbelief.

Though there was something else in her tone that made him feel he should tread warily. He just couldn't put his finger on what that *something* was.

'That there could be a repeat of what happened between us, in Chile.'

'I understood what you were referring to,' she managed stiffly. '*Sex*. You can use the word, Nikhil, I'm not prudish.'

No, she wasn't. A reel of X-rated images rolled through his head, from the unabashed way she'd come apart in his arms to the wild way she'd shattered under his tongue. All of which threatened to break his resolve.

His body was heating at the mere memory, his heart beginning to drum out a beat in his chest. Low, and deep, and carnal. A call to action.

She was so close that he could smell the fresh scent of her shampoo, stirring his memories and telling him that she'd only recently emerged from the shower. Giving him a whole new set of images to contend with. Testing his apparently already fragile resolve.

'Sex then,' he growled, fascinated at the way she fought not to react.

'Sex,' she managed, and it was all he could do not to bend his head and lick the promise-laden word from her lips. 'We had it. And it was... fine.'

'Fine?' The exclamation was out before he could stop it.

'*Good*, then,' she amended. 'But you're mistaken if you think that I spend my days dreaming of more.'

'Indeed?'

Without really knowing what he was doing, Nikhil edged closer to her, ignoring the voice in his head shouting that this was the perfect way out. It allowed Isla to save face whilst giving him what he wanted—what he *said* he wanted—*distance*. It wasn't a challenge; he shouldn't take it as one.

'You don't think of it at all?' His voice sounded odd. Not himself.

'No.' Her voice was insubstantial. 'Never.'

Before he could think better of it, he dipped his head to her ear.

'Liar,' he murmured. 'You want a lot more.'

'No.' She jerked her head a little, as though trying to shake it. 'You're not the only one with no-go rules about colleagues.'

'I'm not talking about other colleagues, Isla. I'm talking about you and me.'

'There is no you and me.' She didn't even sound as if she believed her own words. 'And I don't want there to be.'

'Is that so?'

It took Nikhil all of his willpower not to throw her over his shoulder, carry her to her bed and prove to them both just how weak that declaration was. But he couldn't. He *wouldn't.*

He should never have come here.

He should have gone to the gym and gone several rounds with the punchbag, or run a decent half marathon on the treadmill, or even swum a couple of miles in one of the ship's special lap pools.

Anything to expend energy—and frustration—and to stop himself from coming here.

He should leave now—only he didn't. He stayed rooted to the spot, pretending that he didn't sense his renowned self-control starting to slip away.

The roar grew in Nikhil's head the longer he stood, looking at Isla. Watching the way her pulse jumped in her elegant neck, belying the calm exterior she was so desperately trying to present. That telling, hungry darkening in her glorious eyes. The way her breathing grew as choppy as the seas could around here.

She wanted him. Every bit as much as he wanted her.

Blood pooled in his sex, telling him what it wanted in no uncertain terms. His body at war with his brain. And there was nothing more to it than sex. There couldn't be.

He wouldn't *allow* there to be.

'What do you want from me, Nikhil?' she cried out suddenly.

'Nothing,' he rasped. 'And too much.'

Then, before either of them could analyse that any further, he pressed her up against the wall of her cabin and claimed her mouth with his. And, even as she emitted a weak moan of protest, her arms came up to loop around his neck and press her soft, warm breasts against his chest, their peaks already hard, making his palms itch.

Making every inch of him itch. And ache. And *need*.

She was driving him crazy.

He lifted his hands to her head, taking it gently in his palms and tilting it so that he could better kiss her. He revelled in the way her lips parted when he slicked his tongue over them, inviting him inside, making them both want more.

He kissed her thoroughly, completely, the way he'd wanted to since…for ever. He finally permitted his hands to trail over her body, reacquainting himself with all those mouth-watering curves that haunted him each and every night.

It was sheer bliss to finally give into this dark need to reach around the back of his neck and take her hands, intertwining her fingers with his as he held them against the wall above her head, making her arch into him all the more.

Then, as he encircled both her wrists with one of his hands, he moved his other hand down to relearn the lines of her face, the long sweep of her back and the indent of her waist. All so strangely familiar, as though he'd caressed them a thousand times instead of just that one night.

Or as though he knew them by instinct.

The same instinct that made him lift his hand to the underside of her breast, the sublimity of her heart as it thundered wildly beneath his palm. Betraying her. Confirming everything that he already knew.

Walking his fingers slowly higher, Nikhil allowed his thumb to graze the hard peak, evident even through the material of her uniform. Her harsh intake of breath only fuelling the fires that much more as she let her head tip back to allow his mouth access to her neck, and that sensitive hollow at her throat. And he took full advantage.

It was impossible to resist any longer. He could feel the monster inside him rattling to be let out. To take what he wanted, when what he wanted was Isla. To hell with all his rules and boundaries; she'd been breaking them all from the moment they'd met, anyway.

Sliding his hand down her belly to her abdomen, and lower, Nikhil deftly unbuttoned her crisp white trousers and slid the zip down with a shocking, thrilling sound.

'What…are you doing?' Each word caught deliciously.

But Nikhil didn't have time to dwell. He felt raw, and edgy. Primal. Even as he grazed his teeth over the smooth white of her throat, his fingers buried themselves in her heat. He could barely trust himself to think, let alone speak.

'Giving you what you want,' he managed to grate out.

She gasped softly. 'What about you?'

'Definitely what I want,' he confessed harshly. And then he set about proving it.

CHAPTER EIGHT

IT WAS AN explosion of sensation, tearing through her like the hottest, most blinding light. Everything in her pulled taut. Perfect.

'So wet,' Nikhil muttered, his voice almost reverent.

And Isla let the dark, greedy heat close around them both, like a fist. Her sex flooded with need as he stroked her, slowly at first, taking time to build the pace, making her mindless. The more she bucked against his hand, the lower that growl of laughter, so deep in his throat. But he didn't stop, he didn't even react, his fingers just kept moving exactly where she needed him most, that lazy, leisurely pace that she found so ridiculously addictive.

Yet it wasn't the physical act that affected Isla the most. More, it was the knowledge that Nikhil, with his reputation for being so in control amongst his staff, seemed to consistently show her a different side to himself.

And surely it wasn't too arrogant to think that it could only be *because* it was her?

But there was no time to voice it, or even consider it. His fingers were sliding over her, sending her off into spirals of pleasure. In ten years together, Bradley had never once made her feel this incredible, this on the edge, this desired.

Perhaps worse than that, however, was the fact that she didn't think she'd ever cared. Yet right now, with Nikhil, it was all she could think about. The feel of his fingers playing with her, toying with her. And that incredible wave of sensation, swelling deep inside her, bigger, and higher, like a tsunami of lust until suddenly she realised that it was curling back around—so powerful and so fast—that she barely had time to cling hold of Nikhil before it began to crash over her.

And all she could hear were her own greedy sounds, as she was caught up in the most perfect wipe-out she thought she had ever known.

Isla had no idea how long it took her to resurface. She didn't particularly care. All she knew was that Nikhil was still there, holding her. And that she was desperate for him to feel a fraction of the fervour that he'd just rained down upon her.

She wanted to hear him call out her name, the way he always made her cry out his. And maybe that realisation should scare her more than it did. But, right in that moment, Isla couldn't bring herself to care.

'Now me,' she whispered shakily, one hand still clinging to his shoulder for support, as the other hand slid down his uniform to cup him where he was hard, and ready.

Just for her.

The knock at the door could hardly have been timed much worse.

The atmosphere in the room flipped in a heartbeat as Nikhil wrenched himself away from her, leaving her fighting to stay standing on her still-weak legs. But not before she'd seen the expression in his eyes harden, and she knew he'd shut her out—just as she'd been prising away those defences that he kept around him, like armour.

'Dr Sinclair?'

Another sharp rap seemed to echo through her room.

'Answer them,' Nikhil commanded quietly, his fury barely restrained.

But she knew it was directed more at himself than anyone else. Not that it made the situation any less awkward.

'And say what?' she hissed, relieved her voice didn't quake the way she had feared it might.

'Buy yourself enough time to sort your uniform out, then open the door,' and then he turned and stalked across her room towards the little seated area with the couch.

'I...' She faltered uncertainly, then lifted her voice as confidently as she dared. 'One moment, please.'

Hastily, she fixed her uniform, hoping that Nikhil couldn't see just how badly her hands were shaking. Nonsense, really, when she thought of the way he'd just made her shatter around his mere fingers.

But it didn't matter anyway, because he still had his back to her, apparently searching for something. Her brain couldn't even begin to deal with him right now.

Taking a step forward, she opened the door and a crew member she didn't recognise stared back at her.

'I'm Dr Sinclair,' Isla offered when the girl didn't speak.

'I...is my friend,' she managed at last in broken English. 'He is...ill.'

'If he's ill, then you should call the medical centre.' Isla smiled gently.

The girl looked unexpectedly horrified. 'No... no medical centre...please.'

'I see,' Isla said, frowning.

Alarm bells were going off in her head. If

they didn't want the medical centre alerted, the chances were it was drug-related and they were hoping that, as the new doc on board, she was the weak link.

'Step in, please,' Nikhil's voice commanded evenly, making them both jump. 'Let's not have this conversation in the corridor.'

Isla felt for the young girl as her face paled, and they both looked around the door to where Nikhil was sitting on her couch with a pile of papers on the coffee table in front of him, looking for all the world as though they had been conducting a meeting.

It seemed the crew member wasn't to know that professional meetings didn't generally take place in cabins. Or perhaps she was just too distracted with her own medical emergency to think. Either way, she began backing away from the door.

'No...no, no doctor emergency. Mistake,' she repeated rapidly.

Nikhil was by the door in a flash. 'No mistake,' he told her firmly. 'If someone is sick, whatever the circumstances, he needs to be treated. Dr Sinclair is coming now. You will take us straight to him.'

'No... I...'

'Ready, Dr Sinclair?'

Grabbing her medical bag, Isla pulled the door closed behind them.

'Ready,' she confirmed, waiting for the now terrified girl to turn around before mouthing to Nikhil to alert the medical centre.

They both knew that if drugs were involved then he, and the ship's security, would need to know. However, Isla couldn't help thinking that Nikhil turning up initially would be counter-productive. With a First Officer there, the other crew members—if any of them had hung around long enough—would be more likely to clam up, and Isla feared not learning what the patient had taken.

Besides, the faster someone got to him with a full medical kit, the better. Her bag didn't have that much in it.

She was grateful that Nikhil appeared to re-alise this, turning down a different corridor to head in another direction, leaving the crewmember visibly sighing with relief.

It took several minutes for Isla to reach her patient, even hurrying down the main motorway corridor of the crew decks. But then, finally, they rounded a corner and she saw a cluster of crew around the door to one of the tiny cabins, her fear heightening as they all scattered the moment they saw her.

'There…' The crew member pointed, redundantly.

Pushing her way into the tiny space, Isla finally saw her patient. He was lying on his side, his breathing extremely shallow, his body twitching now and then but otherwise unconscious. A quick measure of his pulse confirmed it was reduced, whilst a check of his eyes confirmed the pupils were constricted. At least someone had had the sense to put him into the recovery position.

Briefly, she checked his airway. Clear—that was good.

'What did he take?'

She didn't really need to hear it, but she asked all the same. Still, it wasn't really a surprise when no one answered.

'The more information I have, the better I am able to treat your friend,' she continued conversationally, biting back her frustration. 'Your loyalty won't count for much if he dies.'

'Skag,' a male voice bit out suddenly. 'Just a bit of Skag.'

Just a bit said it all really, Isla thought, swallowing down a sudden wave of anger. Still, at least it meant she knew the best way to treat him.

'You can treat…yes?' someone asked, their

accent so strong that it took Isla a moment to work out the words.

'I need more kit. You have to alert the medical centre.'

This time no one argued. Though no one moved to do anything either.

'I'm not here to play judge and jury; I just want to help your friend.'

'Fine...' Another voice spoke, and Isla thought it was the same man. 'I'll go.'

'Just call them.' Isla fought to keep her voice even.

'No need.' There was a sudden flurry of activity by the door as Jordanna pushed her way through. 'I'm here.'

Isla eyed the med bag, oxygen cannister and mask with relief.

'That was fast,' she noted.

'Was it? Good, I felt like I went round in circles for a while, asking about a hundred people if they knew anything.'

Isla grunted. 'No one ever wants to be seen to be associated with it. Did you bring Naloxone?'

'Ah, that's what it is, is it? Yeah. I have that.'

'Great.' Isla concentrated on getting in a cannula whilst Jordanna dealt with the oxygen mask. They would need to support respiration with a bag-valve mask before she began to administer the opioid receptor antagonist.

'I thought it was Naltrexone?' a male crewman asked suddenly. Tellingly, Isla thought.

'No—' she lifted her head '—Naltrexone is used to treat drug addiction by blocking opioid cravings, and alcohol cravings for that matter, but it can't treat overdoses. Naloxone can treat the overdose but not the craving.'

The two might sound alike, but their different half-lives really made the distinction. Not that she thought the crewmen wanted that much information.

'Okay, let's start with nought point nought four milligrams—' Isla prepped the syringe '—and see how that goes. Be ready for them.' As soon as the medication hit the brain and began to reverse the effects of the overdose, Isla knew the patient could lash out.

Carefully, she administered the drug.

'What happened to you?' Gerd demanded as he walked into the medical centre a few hours later to see Jordanna on the couch with an ice pack on her eye.

'She got belted by an ungrateful patient.'

'Ah—' the senior nurse nodded '—I heard about that.'

'Already?' Jordanna lifted the pack up and winced.

'You know how news travels fast,' Isla noted, carefully taking her colleague's hand and placing the pack back down over the eye. 'And that kind of news travels even faster.'

'Yeah, well, he'll be escorted off the ship as soon as we get into port, and he'll never work for Port-Star again.' Gerd blew out with satisfaction. 'The security staff will be here any minute to take a statement.'

'Ah, speak of the devil,' Jordanna added, as they heard voices heading up the corridor.

All too familiar voices, Isla realised, as Nikhil's rich tones infiltrated the room. She froze, part of her wanting to flee, the other part knowing she would need to give her report.

She didn't dare look at either Jordanna or Gerd; nonetheless she waited, her heart jumping in her chest, but neither of them said anything more. Apparently, the grapevine hadn't included anything about Nikhil having been in her cabin, and for that she was eternally grateful.

And then Nikhil and the security guard were heading through the surgery doors, and she just about had time to plaster a cheery smile on her face.

'How's the eye, Nurse?' Nikhil asked at once,

and Isla couldn't help smiling as Jordanna practically glowed at the concern.

'I'll survive.'

'Glad to hear it. Are you up to giving your statement?'

'Sure.' The ravishing American flashed a killer smile despite the black eye, but Nikhil had already turned away, leaving her with the equally tall, equally dark, but not quite as handsome security guy.

Jordanna's smile faded for a second and Isla almost felt sorry for her. *Almost.*

But then Nikhil's razor gaze turned on her, and she had to concentrate on radiating a nonchalance she simply didn't feel.

'Doctor—' his tone was courteous, strictly business, and still it sent goosebumps through her '—I appreciate surgery has overrun, but I just need a brief word, please.'

'Of course.' Dipping her head slightly, Isla stood.

'Is your consultation room free?'

Nodding, Isla paced across the reception and into her space, closing the door as Nikhil followed her.

'How many of them were taking it?' he demanded without preamble.

'I don't know.'

'No other medical incidents?'

'Only that one crewman,' Isla confirmed. 'Though I assumed you'd be running a random drugs test.'

'The security team are doing it as we speak, though I'd be grateful for any further information you can provide.'

'I can't,' she apologised. 'I don't know who the other crewmen were; I've never seen them before. In any case, I was too focused on trying to keep my patient alive.'

'I appreciate that.'

'Do you?' she challenged quietly. 'Only it sounds to me as though you're hacked off that I can't give you names.'

For a moment he watched her.

'Where drugs are concerned, we operate a zero-tolerance policy on board our ships. I just don't like people flouting the rules.'

'I'm a doctor, Nikhil, I've seen what this stuff can do to a person. Trust me, I'm the last person you need to lecture on *zero tolerance*.'

He eyed her a moment longer and she resisted the urge to lift her hand to smooth her hair. Or her shirt. Or anything.

'You're right,' he acknowledged at last. 'You're a good doctor, Isla. You should find it easy to get a transfer.'

'Sorry, what did you say?' Taking an inadvertent step back, Isla stared at him in shock.

'You must see that we can't both be on this ship.'

'Why?' Her laugh was too high, too harsh. 'Because I can't tell you who else was involved in whatever happened down on deck five today?'

'Of course not.' He blew out a deep breath and raked his hand through his hair. It was a gesture Isla had never seen from him before, and it threw her for a moment.

'Then what?'

'We got caught, Isla. Right now, that crew member is in shock about her friend. But soon enough she'll put two and two together.'

'I don't agree.' Isla fought back the wave of fear that was beginning to flood her. 'You handled it well, Nikhil. You made it look like it was a genuine work meeting.'

'*This* time,' he emphasised. 'But what happens next time? Or the time after? When do too many coincidences add up?'

And it would only be later—much later— that Isla would consider the hidden relevance to Nikhil's words. The truth that he no doubt hadn't intended for her to see, that he craved more of her, just as she did of him.

But in that moment she wasn't thinking straight.

'So what do you expect me to do?' Isla let out a sharp laugh. 'Put in for a transfer?'

The silence swirled around them, as shocking as it was unbelievable. In the end it was Nikhil who spoke first.

'You must see that we can't stay on this ship together without risking both our reputations?'

'You expect *me* to transfer,' she breathed quietly.

'You were never meant to be on this ship in the first place,' bit out Nikhil. 'You were supposed to be on the *Jewel of Hestia*. That night would never have happened if I'd known you would end up here.'

Isla didn't know what made her stand up taller and pull her shoulders back. Some belated sense of self-preservation, perhaps.

'It wouldn't have happened if *I* had known we would end up being on the same ship,' she declared. 'But here I am. And I'm not going anywhere.'

'I came here to offer a solution, not to argue.'

He actually looked as though he believed it, and Isla almost laughed. Instead, she fought to bite back her frustration.

'Then don't say stupid things.'

He cast her a disapproving look, and she hated the way it made her feel inferior. Wanting.

'I would rather do this with civility, Isla.'

A lesser person might have trembled at the lethal quality to his tone, despite the silkiness, or the actual words used. But Isla refused to be that *lesser person*. Not any more.

'Or what?' she asked, cocking her head to one side. 'Are you going to threaten me?'

'No threat.' How did he manage to smile in such a way that she could practically feel his teeth, sharp against her skin? 'Just forewarning you.'

'Forewarning me?'

'If you don't put in for a transfer, then I shall have to request one for you. As your senior officer.'

'On what grounds?' Isla demanded incredulously. 'I've done nothing wrong.'

He couldn't do that, surely? He *wouldn't*.

'I wouldn't suggest that you had.'

'But the very fact that you ask for me to be transferred will raise suspicion.' Isla threw her hands into the air, her composure beginning to fray.

'Which is why I suggest that *you* put in for the transfer. Tell them you want to go back to a smaller ship. Tell them you aren't ready for a ship like the *Cassiopiea*.'

'You wouldn't dare,' she replied, fury slamming through her. 'That will sit on my record. It would affect my chances of promotion in the future.'

'I'll write you a glowing reference.'

'Dr Turner would write me a glowing reference. He is, after all, my direct boss. But it's irrelevant, because I'm not doing it.' She folded her arms over her chest.

Fury was beginning to override everything else right now, and for that she was grateful.

'There's nothing you can say, Nikhil. Sleeping with the First Officer might be frowned upon, but it happened off-ship, before we even knew that we would be colleagues.'

'What happened this afternoon wasn't *off-ship*.'

'No, but it was also after *you* came to *my* cabin,' Isla bit out. 'And if you insist on trying to get me transferred and interfering in my career then I'll have no choice than to tell people.'

'You're threatening me?' He glared at her in disbelief, something black and deadly crossing his features. Enough to make her skin prickle with awareness. 'To tell people I... What? Coerced you?'

'Of course not.' Isla was horrified. 'But the fact is, it wouldn't have happened if you hadn't come to my cabin. So, I'm not torpedoing my career just because this…attraction between us is so strong that you gave into temptation once and let your ridiculous high standards for yourself slip.'

'Twice.'

'What?'

'I let my personal boundaries slip twice,' he grated out. And suddenly Isla realised that Nikhil's battle was more with himself than with her. 'The first time was the other day when I kissed you in the damned corridor.'

'No one even saw.'

'But they could have,' he growled.

'But they didn't,' she repeated. But it was too late.

She could feel the rage and the hurt swirling inside her, and they made for a lethal combination.

'I'll tell you what, Nikhil Dara,' she threw at him, 'you stay away from me, and I'll stay the hell away from you.'

Then, before either of them could say anything further, she yanked open the door and stalked outside on legs she was sure would buckle under her at any moment. If only staying away from Nikhil was that easy.

If only her need for him didn't pump through her veins like a drug. Turning her into something all too close to that idiot patient in the crew rooms earlier.

Only Nikhil wanted her too. Just as badly. And if what had just happened was his attempt at intimidation then it had done exactly the opposite of everything he'd intended, because it didn't tell her that he regretted what had happened between them that first night in Chile.

It told her that he couldn't trust himself not to be tempted to do the same again. And being that desired by Nikhil Dara was a heady experience indeed.

CHAPTER NINE

THE KNOCK ON her door several hours later made Isla's heart lurch violently in her chest. Enough to leave a mark.

Nikhil.

It was all she could do not to race across the room and yank it open. She would *not* be the infatuated girl who fell all over him just because he'd changed his mind and chosen to bestow his time and attention on her.

With deliberate care, she walked to the door, placed her fingers over the handle and drew in a deep breath. She'd barely unlocked it when it was pushed open and a figure was sweeping past her, inside.

'Good grief, this hovel can't possibly be your cabin!'

Isla stared for a moment, horrified. 'What are you doing here, Mother?'

Marianna spun around dramatically, her arms outstretched. 'I came to see you, my darling. To make sure you were all right. I missed you that last night in Chile. We were going to have such a good evening together, but you had to go and get yourself transferred onto an earlier ship.'

Hardly how it had been, but Isla knew better than to argue with her mother over trivial things. She'd long since learned to save her energy for the bigger issues. Like how her mother was *here*.

'So you booked yourself a last-minute cabin on my ship?'

No need to ask her mother how much that had cost. It wasn't as though money was an issue to Marianna. No doubt she'd flown in from Chile by helicopter, with the top concierge standing out there on the landing pad to greet her. Her mother was a master at making an entrance.

Especially when Marianna was grinning at her like that. That was to say that a lesser woman might have *grinned*. Her mother *dazzled*.

'It occurred to me that it might be fun, my flower. Don't tell me you aren't pleased to see me?'

Isla opened her mouth, then closed it again as a smile tugged at the corners of her lips. No matter how frustrating her mother was, it was impossible not to be drawn to such a wild, charismatic personality. If nothing else, her mother was never predictable.

'Besides, you know I always enjoy a good cruise. Now, come and give me a hug.'

Dutifully, Isla stepped over to her mother and allowed herself to be enveloped in a tight embrace. Familiar, and somehow oddly comforting.

'Of course it's good to see you.' She pulled her head back and shot Marianna a warning look. 'Just don't interfere in my job.'

'Of course not!' Her mother had long since perfected the butter-wouldn't-melt look, not that Isla bought it for a moment.

'I mean it, Mother,' Isla reiterated. For all the good that would do.

Marianna had always been headstrong, wanting the best for herself, and for Isla.

'It's like talking to a metal bulkhead.' Isla rolled her eyes. 'Where's Leo, anyway?'

'Forgive a mother for wanting a moment to catch up with her other beautiful girl.' Marianna rolled her eyes, but they twinkled all the same. 'If only you'd been quite so delighted to see me.'

'I am,' Isla argued. 'You know I am.'

Her mother waved her hand dismissively.

'Anyway, Leo isn't here. She met someone.'

'*Leo* met someone? Wait—you seem remarkably smug about it. You set her up, didn't you? Oh, *Mother.*'

'It was purely fortuitous, I can assure you.'

Realisation walloped Isla. Clear and unequivocal.

'You've come to set *me* up with someone, haven't you?'

'Of course not.' For the second time in as many moments, Marianna flashed her an innocent look.

And for the second time in as many moments, Isla refused to be fooled; she'd seen her mother wield it as both a shield and a weapon for years.

'Mother, I am here to find myself as a doctor, the way I always wanted to do. Not to find myself a husband, the way *you* always wanted me to do.'

'You're here to lick your wounds after Bradley,' her mother corrected. 'But he simply isn't worth the upset.'

'I can assure you, Mother, I don't care in the least about Brad-the-Cad.'

'Well, of course, darling. Glad to hear it.'

But at least Marianna had the grace to look sheepish.

'Right.' Isla eyed her mother cautiously. 'Just as long as you understand that.'

'Oh, I do.'

It was all too suspiciously easy. Warily, Isla

closed the door behind them. She might have known it was too good to be true.

'Although, if the opportunity with some eligible male should present itself, grab it by the... horns, I always say.'

'Mother...' Isla chastised.

'It's come to my attention that you have a very nice First Officer on board, by the name of Nikhil Dara,' Marianna noted, her expression too casual.

'What do you know about Nikhil?' Isla breathed, realising her mistake too late.

Her mother eyed her shrewdly. 'How very interesting.'

Isla kicked herself. She knew her mother well enough to have known not to react. Marianna was too sharp by half.

'Mother...'

'I know that Leo is off with Daksh Dara. Not that she thinks I know it.'

'*Daksh* Dara?'

'He calls himself Dax, and he is Nikhil's older brother.'

'Nikhil's brother is still alive??' Isla exclaimed.

'Very much so?',' Marianna noted, and it took a moment for Isla to realise that her mother was watching her a little too closely. 'Why? Did he tell you otherwise?'

'Yes,' Isla managed. Then she stopped, and shook her head. 'Actually, no. He told me that he lost his brother a long time ago. I just…assumed.'

'I see.' Her mother arched her perfect eyebrows. 'Well, Nikhil's brother was certainly alive and well the last time we met. But they "are" estranged, from what I've been able to work out.'

'From what you can work out?'

'She met him when you two were in Chile together. In fact, he was the one I was trying to set you up with, that last night.'

Isla shook her head, utterly confused. *In Chile? When she had met Nikhil?*

'He never said. He never… I didn't even know his brother was alive.' She glanced up at her mother. 'So that's why you're really here? To find out about Nikhil and…this Daksh?'

Her mother hesitated a beat, then shrugged. 'You and Leo are precious to me.' She offered a soft smile. 'You know how I think of her as much my daughter as you are.'

'I know.' Isla returned the smile instantly. 'It just… She met this Daksh in Chile, when Nikhil was there?'

'I understood that the two men were meant to be meeting. Something about a birthday?'

'Nikhil said it was his birthday…' Isla snapped her head up sharply. 'He took me for a meal at

Te Tinca, but he never mentioned anything about meeting anyone.'

Clamping her mouth shut, Isla hoped her mother didn't probe her further on that point. Which meant she was surprised when Marianna closed the gap between them and, placing her hands gently on either side of Isla's face, upturned it so that she could look into her daughter's eyes.

'My eyes don't deceive me, Isla. You're blushing, and you never blush.'

Isla opened her mouth to object, but abruptly shut it again. There was little point in pretending to her mother. Not where men were concerned.

'It isn't what you think,' Isla offered at length. 'Can we just leave it at that?'

'If that's what you want.'

Isla chewed on her lip for a moment.

'It's…complicated.'

'Then let me just say three things. One, tonight I'm invited to the Captain's invitation-only gala ball, and you are my guest. Two, this man Nikhil makes you blush and I never, not once, saw you blush with that idiot Bradley. And three, never forget that beneath the Sinclair you're also a Raleigh, which gives you an impressive armoury of practically perfect genes at your fingertips. And the ability to use them.'

Then she dropped her hands and swept towards the door without a backward glance.

Nikhil wasn't entirely certain that he'd manage to stay standing when he looked up from his conversation with the Captain to see Isla standing at the gala entrance, a vision in the deepest, most glorious red. Her golden-brown hair tumbled down over her shoulders like a glossy curtain, caressing her skin in a way that made his body ache to do the same.

And that was without taking into account the way the gown hung from one shoulder, making love to her curves as it dropped, until it fell in a cascade of reds to another pair of killer heels.

Judging by the expressions on a fair few of his colleagues' faces, they were thinking the same, and yet when she looked into the room, her eyes colliding with his—and holding—he felt the most forceful punch of triumph.

It was impossible to tear his glance away. A point which was made clear when he heard the Captain coughing pointedly in his ear.

'I take it the rumours are true, Nikhil.'

It took Nikhil every bit of willpower he had to drag his gaze from Isla.

'Say again, sir?'

'I didn't believe them. Not until now. But there

really is something going on between you and the doctor, isn't there?'

'You know me, sir.' Nikhil gritted his teeth. 'All work, no play.'

'It's served you well,' the Captain agreed. 'But a word of advice. The last time I saw someone wear that expression was when I looked in the mirror the first time I realised I was in love with my wife.'

'I am certainly not in love with Dr Sinclair.'

'That was thirty years ago,' the older man continued, as if Nikhil hadn't even spoken. 'And she is still the only woman I have ever looked at that way. Even since she died there has been no one else. So if you care about that woman over there, Nikhil, I suggest you do something about it. Before one of these other blokes around here decides she's fair game.'

Nikhil clamped his jaws together so hard that it was almost painful. But he refused to let anyone see how his old mentor's words got to him. He refused to show any weakness. And these... *feelings* he had for Isla Sinclair were surely a weakness.

'And, you know, it couldn't have come at a more fortuitous time, actually,' the Captain confided suddenly.

'Is that so?'

Nikhil didn't really want to know. He didn't care. He just wanted to end the conversation so that he could go over and wrap her arm through his—staking his claim on her in front of all these would-be suitors, like a damned dog marking its territory.

'One of the other fleet Captains is retiring at the end of the year. We've all been asked to put forward potential candidates for promotion. I wanted to put you forward.'

'You *wanted* to?' Nikhil frowned, his mind struggling to keep up, when all it really wanted to do was snap straight back to the woman across the room.

'I have no doubt that you're the best officer for the role, Nikhil, but Head Office prefer their Captains to be married, or widowed. They don't like single, even one as dedicated and professional as you.'

Finally, Nikhil's gaze stopped trying to fight its way back to Isla. He stared at the Captain. 'You're saying that they wouldn't consider me for promotion without a wife?'

'Archaic, isn't it?' The older man shrugged. 'The one thing you've avoided all this time is going to be the thing that gets you the promotion you've been working for, your entire career.'

Nikhil watched her move. Her lithe body

rippling under the sequinned fabric, arresting heads—and other, more carnal parts of the male anatomy. She was magnificent. Incomparable and, apparently, the key to getting everything he'd ever wanted.

His own ship.

So why did he know, without even thinking about it, that there was no way he could use her like that? He'd been fighting their attraction because he'd always prided himself on his professionalism, yet it seemed that resisting temptation would be his downfall, not his success.

So why not give in to it? Why not give in to Isla, and gain two things in the process?

Because she deserves better than that, a voice insinuated itself into his head. And he didn't exactly try to silence it.

Instead, he watched as she circled the room, apparently doing all she could to avoid moving to the point where he stood, still with the Captain. Now she was with the woman who declared herself to be Isla's mother.

He could certainly see the resemblance. The high, fine bone structure, the delicate nose and those oh-so-expressive eyes. But Marianna had a worldliness to her that Isla didn't possess. And though they both had an intelligent sharpness in their gaze, he could read the honed intellect in

Isla's expression that simply wasn't present in that of her mother.

For over an hour he watched her move between guests, charming people and laughing with them, and he told himself that he didn't feel jealous, or possessive, or indeed anything at all.

He wasn't sure that he fell for it, for a moment.

And then, suddenly, she was right in front of him and every cell in his body *zinged* with awareness.

'Nikhil, I want to introduce you to my mother, Marianna Sinclair-Raleigh-Burton. Mother, this is Nikhil Dara.'

'Nikhil Dara.' Isla's mother held her hand out for him to take as he smiled politely, wholly unprepared for the blow he was about to suffer. 'Surely no relation to the delightful Daksh Dara of DXD Industries?'

Isla had no idea why she was standing there, unable to breathe, as Nikhil and her mother stood face to face, each weighing up the other in their different ways.

Her mother on one side, as glittery and charming as ever on the outside, but with the lethal blade of a smile that only Isla knew was being wielded as a weapon. And Nikhil on the other, a hard edge to his body that she'd never seen before, an expression she couldn't read playing across his harsh features.

There was no reason for her to have wished so fervently that things would go well between the two of them during these introductions, and yet that was exactly how she'd felt.

It had been like some insane torture, watching Nikhil from across the room and not being able to talk to him for fear of betraying every one of these bizarre, hectic feelings that swirled inside her. Despite everything she'd said about staying away from each other.

It didn't matter where she went, or where *he* went for that matter, she seemed to be constantly aware of him. Helpless to stop herself from tracking his movements around the room. Telling herself that she was just imagining the fact that he was deliberately avoiding her. She probably didn't even factor into his consideration at all, as he moved from group to group, playing the eligible yet professional First Officer to perfection.

But *he* factored into *her* consideration.

She felt perpetually on edge. On fire. As if there was a burning in her chest that roared louder the nearer he came. It thrummed through her veins, humming along her entire body, leaving her aching…right *there*.

Wanting him with a hunger she'd never experienced before. Ever. And it didn't seem to matter how many times she told herself that she was acting crazily, she couldn't seem to stop herself. It was as if a maelstrom of emotions was raging inside her and Nikhil was at the very centre of it.

Her only saving grace was the fact that no one knew her well enough to see that. And she couldn't work out if that was particularly lucky, or particularly sad.

Yet now here she was, at a Captain's gala with her mother and the man she couldn't stop thinking about—fantasising about—and they were eyeing each other like sworn enemies. Surely the last couple of minutes couldn't have gone any worse? Like some kind of terrible nightmare.

'You're not at all like your brother, are you?' Marianna spoke.

'I am not.' Nikhil's voice scraped over Isla, though she couldn't have said why. 'One of us is the exemplary, irreproachable Dara brother; the other is the Dara brother whose moral standing lies in tatters on the ground. We are not to be confused with each other.'

Isla tried to speak, to somehow shatter the tension of the moment, but all she could do was watch the scene unfold with increasing horror. This car crash of an introduction that she couldn't seem to avert; that shouldn't even matter to her. Finally, she watched her mother slip her arm through the Captain's—who had come to the rescue like some kind of perfect white knight in his ship's uniform—and the two of them wandered off.

She waited until they were out of earshot.

'What the hell was that all about?'

Nikhil turned to face her and she was sure she saw a brief flash of regret in his eyes before he switched up a blank expression.

'I believe your mother observed how dissimilar my brother and I are. I merely agreed.'

She wasn't sure why, but she had never felt so much like crying. Not even when she'd discovered how Brad had been using her. Using her connections, and her money, to get to where he wanted to be. Some might argue that was just the way her mother had behaved, with her series of husbands. The difference was that her mother had never feigned love.

Bradley had. And she'd been the damned fool who had believed him.

Which only made it all the more laughable that she'd actually heeded her mother's advice for once and dressed tonight with Nikhil in mind.

Not *for* him, she had told herself as she'd stood in front of the mirror, eyeing her reflection critically. But with him in mind, all the same. Going against the last thing she'd flung at him, about staying away from each other—because she'd thought that she'd begun to understood a little more of what made him tick.

And now she might as well be looking at a stranger.

'You deliberately made yourself sound like... like...someone else. Someone I don't recognise.'

'No.' His voice was harsh. Much too harsh, Isla thought faintly. 'I didn't make myself sound like anyone else. This is who I am, Isla. You just don't know me at all.'

'I know that wasn't you.' She held her ground.

'You know no such thing.'

'Is this because she asked about your brother?' Isla had no idea why that popped into her brain, but suddenly there it was.

And even though Nikhil didn't respond, the sudden set of his jaw and coldness in his eyes was answer enough. Also, oddly, there was a bleakness to his expression which made her heart twist for him, even as she didn't understand why.

Before she could say another word, Nikhil had taken her by the elbow and was manoeuvring her out of the ballroom and into an anteroom.

'What the hell do you know about Daksh?' Nikhil rasped. 'Did your socially climbing mother think I was her route to him? *Your* route to him?'

'I didn't even know he existed until tonight,' Isla managed, valiantly holding back the tremors that threatened to roll through her body like its own version of seismic activity.

'I told you I had a brother,' Nikhil cut her off.

'You made him sound like he was dead,' she cried.

His stony expression seemed to harden even further beneath her gaze. His voice all the more implaccable.

'Is that what you're going to claim?'

'It's the truth. And anyway, my mother didn't know I had met you back in Chile, least of all that I spent that night with you.'

'And I am to believe that?'

And finally—*finally*—she felt that hint of steel inside her that she'd begun to think had deserted her. Grabbing hold of it, she made herself face Nikhil.

'I can't say that I care what you believe,' she heard herself say, although she barely recognised her own voice.

Every sweep of his eyes over her made Isla feel as though she didn't fit her own skin any more. Everything was shifting around her and she couldn't seem to make sense of it. And still she wished, more than anything, that she could read what was going on in Nikhil's head *right now*.

'You were right earlier, Isla,' he growled, out of the blue. 'We should stay the hell away from each other.'

CHAPTER TEN

THE GONDOLA RIDE up through the rainforest canopy had to be one of the most incredible experiences Isla thought she'd ever had. Sloths could be seen, hanging from the higher limbs of stunning towering trees. Bats and brightly coloured birds clung to the enormous leaves and, a few moments earlier, she'd even seen a monkey leaping from tree to tree, as if keeping up with the gondola's ascent.

'…such is the neotropical diversity of this rainforest.'

Isla tuned back in to their tour guide, trying to chastise herself for missing what he was saying. But surely it was impossible not to get caught up in the magical beauty of this place.

'Even to date we are still finding new species in the rainforest,' he continued. 'Especially insects. And now it's time for your aerial zip wire.'

'Not for me—' she laughed '—I'm here as the excursion doctor. That's all.'

'Surely you aren't going to be so disappointing as to bottle it, Dr Sinclair?'

Emotion rushed through her, devastating her. Her heart started pounding, though not in her chest. More like in the vicinity of her throat. And she despaired of herself.

Carefully, Isla steeled herself for the first sight of Nikhil in over a week—ever since that awful night at the Captain's gala. She'd also spent the past week avoiding her mother—not too difficult, since Marianna and the Captain appeared to have hit it off entirely too well that night and, as far as she could tell, her mother had barely been back to her palatial stateroom since.

Taking a deep breath, she slowly—so slowly— turned around…and promptly despaired of herself. How could it be that she *still* wasn't ready for the way her breath whooshed out of her lungs as her eyes seemed to drink in the sight of him?

Worse, when he inclined his head in a wordless instruction for her to move away from the crowd, to the far end of the summit station, she instructed herself that the ludicrous thrill that chased through her right at this moment was revulsion, not some sick kind of pleasure at seeing him again.

And she certainly didn't notice the dark rings around his eyes, or the taut lines by his mouth, as though he hadn't been sleeping much better than she had this last week.

'I'm on duty,' she managed, forcing herself to hold her position and smile. Though most of the group had already descended on the zip wire, there were still a few passengers awaiting their turn and she had absolutely no intention of alerting them to the fact that there was any tension between their doctor and the First Officer. 'I can't stray far from this group.'

'If there's a medical emergency, then the senior tour guide will be alerted on his radio and we'll soon know about it.'

Reluctantly, Isla forced herself to move off to the side with Nikhil, enough that they couldn't be overheard.

'I didn't request this excursion, before you ask. It was another...'

'Another one of your predecessor's choices. Yes, I am aware of that fact. I had the good doctor's trip schedule emailed to me after Ecuador.'

'Of course you did.' She shouldn't be surprised. 'I don't know why I'm surprised.'

'I didn't come here to fight with you, Isla.'

'Did you not?' She raised an eyebrow, safe in the knowledge that the rest of the party couldn't see her. 'I'm agog to know why you did come, then.'

'I came to apologise.'

Isla's heart stopped. She must have misheard. 'Sorry?'

'This is your career too. I should never have asked you to transfer.'

'Then why did you?' She couldn't seem to help herself.

There was a beat of silence, but it felt like a lifetime.

'Perhaps it was an excuse to be with you again,' Nikhil bit out suddenly.

There was no way his words should be able to worm their way inside her so easily.

'Your excuse?'

'I think I probably convinced myself that if you were going to the *Hestia*, the way you'd been intended to do, then we would no longer be immediate colleagues. We could indulge this… attraction between us.'

'There's bed-hopping going on every night. From the lowliest crewman right up to the senior officers. And yet you're worried about us indulging with each other, and only each other?'

She could see the internal battle going on in Nikhil's head. She could read it in every tautened sinew of his impossibly perfect body. But she refused to let her head go there. Not now.

'I never indulge, *Doctor.* You know that.'

'Actually, I don't know that,' she heard herself snap out abruptly. More because his use of *Doctor* made her feel things she didn't want to be feeling. 'I don't know that at all. I've heard rumours, but that's all they are. I don't know the first thing about you, Nikhil.'

'You know me probably better than anyone else on this ship.'

'Then I find that profoundly sad. Not least because I didn't even realise that your brother was still alive. Let alone that you'd been scheduled to meet him in Chile, the day that we met.'

Nikhil stiffened. A lesser woman might have quaked at the incandescent expression on his face. Isla had no idea how she managed to hold her ground.

'How do you know about that?'

'More to the point—' she refused to answer, though it took all she had '—how is it that in all our conversations about my family, you never once offered anything more about yours?'

'It wasn't...isn't your business,' he gritted out. 'It's nobody's business.'

'It's a detail. A minor, insignificant detail perhaps.' She carefully ignored the fact that her mother had told her the brothers were estranged. 'But a detail nonetheless.'

Let Nikhil tell her that. Let him at least acknowledge the fact that Dax existed. And again, he hesitated. So long, this time, that Isla feared he wasn't going to answer her at all.

'Perhaps it's self-preservation,' he growled at last.

'It isn't self-preservation,' she made herself reply. 'It's control. You set up these little parameters around yourself every day. That particular, irrelevant scrap of information was withheld purely because you get some kind of kick about no one knowing the slightest thing about you.'

'And yet I told you it was my birthday,' he reminded her.

Isla faltered. He *had* told her that, hadn't he? And yet she'd assumed he was making it up.

Nikhil was quick to exploit his advantage. 'I didn't tell you about my *brother*—' she was fairly certain he fought to keep his tone even, yet that hint of acrid rage slid through all the same '—because he is irrelevant to me. That is all. No great secret.'

'It's hardly usual,' Isla snorted.

'Many families part ways. Your close relationship with your former stepsister is more unusual than any fallout I may or may not have had with mine.'

'Which, I feel obliged to point out, is you deflecting—' she couldn't decide whether to feel smug or sad '—the way you always do.'

'I disagree.'

'It's *exactly* what you do.' She refused to be swayed. 'In fact, you turn the conversation back on the other person, or you simply dismiss them.'

'You're mistaken,' he began, but whatever else he was going to say was cut off by the low, insistent ring of a mobile. Nikhil's mobile.

As he stepped away to answer, Isla took the opportunity to slip past him and back to the group.

Or, more accurately, she forced her shaking legs to carry her away from him—every step feeling heavier than the last—as she tagged onto the end of the last few passengers waiting to enjoy the thrill of their zip wire experience.

'That was the team back at the hotel base. There's a problem with one of the guests who took the Orchid and Butterfly House tour. They want you back immediately.'

'Understood.' Swinging around, she began to head back to the embarkation point for the gondolas heading back down to the low station.

He caught her as she started to pass him, and it was harder than ever to pretend that the contact didn't do anything to her.

'Where are you going?'

'Back down.' She frowned at him.

'Yes, but not that way.' He turned her around to the zip wire. 'We'll go this way instead. It will be faster.'

'Fine.' She gritted her teeth, telling herself that the jolt that ran through her was solely about the ride. 'Let's go.'

They were just coming into the rainforest hotel when the call came through to say that the patient was fine after all. It had turned out that their broken ankle had healed remarkably fast once they'd been offered an upgrade.

'A few weeks ago, I'd have been shocked,' Isla commented as they slowed down to walk up the beautiful tropical-tree lined driveway.

Sweat was trickling down her back, and her shirt felt heavy with moisture. The place was hot and humid enough, but they'd been practically jogging through dense forest to get back to the hotel.

'Let me guess,' Nikhil said dryly. 'The first few days aboard, you had several new arrivals coming to your surgery crying about being claustrophobic?'

'Only an upgrade to a cabin with a balcony would cure them.' Isla nodded. 'Yes. I truly didn't believe people would do that.'

His only answer was a grunt of disapproval.

She supposed he'd got used to it after so many years, and so many cruises. What kind of a fool did it make her that she still, even now, longed to hear him tell her something more personal about himself?

'There are many more nice passengers, though,' she heard herself add.

Beside her, he seemed to stalk up the drive, but he didn't utter a word.

'And there's a lot to be said for waking up in a new place every morning. I mean, it's a stunning way to get to see the world.'

'Go in the back way,' he gritted out suddenly. 'Those lovely passengers you mentioned will descend on us the moment we walk through the door, and I'd like to at least get a shower and clean up first.'

She didn't dare to look at him. It seemed impossible, but even drenched in sweat he looked like a study in perfect masculinity. Perhaps more so. Moisture glistened on his skin, bronzed and healthy, making him look all the more like some billboard model. Only a more interesting, real version.

Oh, she was in serious trouble.

Following Nikhil as he skirted the main entrance to the hotel, an odd, short, instantly muffled sound made them stop simultaneously. For a protracted second, Isla struggled to work it out—and then her stomach turned. She set off at a run, but Nikhil was already ahead of her.

Rounding the corner of a store house, they saw that a lad, tall and muscled, had a maid pinned to the grubby wooden framework and was tugging her skirt up, despite her futile attempts to push him off.

Before Isla could say anything, Nikhil had placed both his hands on the young man's shoulders and was hauling him off the sobbing girl and swinging him around.

The girl began to scream, and Isla hurried to stop her. The last thing they needed now was for a load of hotel guests to come spilling out to see what was going on.

Turning back to Nikhil and the attacker, she saw the punch coming as if in slow motion, but it was only at the last minute that she saw a glint of metal and then the blood as the lad slashed Nikhil's shoulder.

In an instant the expression on Nikhil's face changed—a flash of a stricken expression, enough to make her blood run cold. It was gone in an instant, but even that fraction of a moment had been long enough to hurl images into Isla's mind—the scars she'd seen on his body that night in Chile. In particular, the one on his shoulder—the one he'd told her had been an accident. Suddenly, she wasn't so sure.

But there was no time to dwell on that now. Her attention was pulled back to Nikhil, who had already reacted, landing a few smart punches to send the blade skittering. He'd swiftly got his opponent against the wall, despite the lad's muscled form, his forearm to the lad's throat to stop him from escaping.

He growled to her, 'Go inside and get a member of security. Be discreet. And take the girl with you.'

She only hesitated for half a second. Then, wordlessly, she obeyed.

However she'd anticipated this day going, it couldn't have been like this. But that moment of barely controlled rage she'd seen on Nikhil's face kept tugging at her thoughts. Years as a doctor had honed her intuition, and right now it was telling her that the knife had triggered something in him, if only for less than a minute.

Her thoughts were still whirring, even as she escorted the trembling, sobbing maid in through the staff-only doors, soothing her as best she could in her broken Spanish.

'I need to clean the wound; it's going to sting,' Isla warned an hour or so later when, statements given, they were in his room, where she could tend to Nikhil without fear of any of the passengers seeing them.

Judging by the laughter and music coming from the main ballroom as she and Nikhil had left the security office, the shore excursions staff were doing their usual sterling job of looking after the ship's passengers.

If they hadn't been happy, no doubt Nikhil would have rushed to clean up and get back to the party, when what he really needed was for his wound to be dealt with—butterfly stitches at least—and a bit of rest. With the canopy tour done and the tour group content, however, neither of them should be needed until the return journey to ship after lunchtime the next day, unless there was a problem.

Instead, the main problem was focusing on the task in hand when Nikhil was sitting in front of her, stripped to the waist, his chiselled body as mouth-watering as ever, and sending every inch of her body into a fever that had nothing to do with the soaring temperature outside.

She really was woeful.

'At least you've had all your tetanus shots, coming out here. Quite a barrage of injections, wasn't it?'

He grunted, but didn't speak.

'It will leave a scar,' Isla heard herself say. 'Though nothing like the one on your shoulder, of course.'

And she didn't know why she carried on—pushing that little bit harder.

'Will you tell people that it's the result of another accident?'

She might as well have struck him herself. Perhaps that was what she'd intended her words to do. Either way, Nikhil stiffened where he sat, and the silence in the room grew heavier in an instant. All she could do was continue to clean the wound and wait.

'I won't tell people anything,' he managed grimly at last. 'No one else will see it.'

She should stop talking. Now. But she couldn't seem to stop herself.

'I saw it.'

Something cracked through the quiet, like a thunderclap, though one glance at the window assured her the sun was still as sweltering out there as before.

'Most women I sleep with are less distracted by any…blemishes—especially those that are perceived. Clearly, I was remiss if some inconsequential childhood scar is what you remember most from our night together. I shall be more… dedicated in future.'

Isla swallowed, heat pouring straight down through her, right to the apex of her legs. Logically, she knew he didn't mean *in the future with her*, and yet it hung there, unspoken, all the same. Her heart faltered and swelled.

'What happened back in your past, Nikhil?' She paused but he didn't answer. Taking a steadying breath, she continued. 'I saw your face when you first caught a glimpse of that lad's knife. Your expression...'

'Leave it be, Isla.' The dark warning in his tone couldn't have been clearer.

And yet she couldn't seem to make her runaway mouth comply.

'Was it Daksh? Is that why you and your brother no longer speak? Why you claim that one of you is irreproachable, whilst the other has been left with no morals? Which one of you is which, Nikhil? Or is that the point?'

She waited for a moment, her agitation increasing as his jaw locked tighter. Angrier. 'I need to know, Nikhil. My stepsister is allegedly with him. If he's dangerous, then I want to know.'

His head snapped around to hers instantaneously, his voice rolling through her like black fury.

'Say that again?'

'Leo—I told you about her—is supposedly with him.'

'How?' The word was like a whip, lashing against Isla's skin. His gaze was boring into her, pinning her to the spot.

'They met in Chile. The day after you and I...' She tailed off awkwardly.

A myriad expressions chased through Nikhil's rich eyes and, to Isla's chagrin, none of them seemed good. But the one she recognised most of all was fury—with *her*.

'And you've known all this time?'

'No.' Isla shook her head. 'I only found out last week—from my mother. Please, Nikhil. Leo means everything to me. If she's in danger, then you have to tell me.'

He glowered at her for another long moment and everything in her was sounding an alarm. And then, finally, he spoke—as though through gritted teeth.

'Daksh was not the one who wielded that knife. Your stepsister is in no danger from him. At least, not physically.'

Relief coursed through her, but she still had to understand.

'What's that supposed to mean? *At least, not physically?*'

He looked as if he wasn't going to answer again, and then he opened his mouth.

'It means he would not physically hurt her. But he is no more capable of an emotional connection than I am. My brother is certainly not to be relied upon.'

And there was no mistaking the bitter tone to Nikhil's voice. But there was something else too. Something less easy to recognise.

Isla nudged at it, as if with her toe.

Hurt. That was what she thought she could see. Whatever had happened between Nikhil and his brother had left Nikhil bitter, and hurt. Yet surely there was no reason for her to find that as interesting as she did? There was no reason for her to cling onto it as though it was another rare find, another precious piece of the Nikhil puzzle.

'So Leo isn't at risk of any harm with Daksh?'

'No,' he bit out. 'You need have no fear over her physical well-being.'

'Well, she's a big girl. In terms of her emotional well-being, she can look out for herself.'

And Isla didn't know if they were still talking about her stepsister.

For another few moments they lapsed back into the same heavy silence. Nikhil's face was set as she made her shaking fingers get back to their work of tending to the laceration on his arm.

She wondered if the cuts on his heart—the deep wounds he pretended didn't exist—could ever be treated as easily. But she didn't dare push him further. She'd clearly already probed too much, and he'd made it perfectly clear that it wasn't any of her business.

As much as that stung, she needed to respect that. For her own sake as much as anything.

Working quickly and efficiently, Isla finished tending to the wound, applying the strips and dressing it so that it didn't risk opening up under the white shirt of his uniform. Finally, satisfied it was done, she stepped back.

'Okay, you're all clear.'

It was harder than it should have been to sound cheerful. And harder still when he stood and turned to face her.

She fought to keep her eyes from travelling down from his chin.

'And thank you for telling me about Daksh. You...didn't have to, but I am grateful.'

He watched her wordlessly until she found herself shifting her weight from one foot to the other.

'Nikhil...'

'You're concerned for someone you care about.' He spoke suddenly. 'You shouldn't feel the need to apologise for that. It must be...nice.'

It was a closed statement. He certainly wasn't inviting a response. Yet, even though the voice in her head was screaming at her to bite her tongue, Isla couldn't help herself from responding.

'Are you sure you don't have someone like that either?'

'I do not.'

'What about your brother? Are you so sure he doesn't care?'

'He does not.'

'So why was he there, in Chile?'

'Careful.' Nikhil's eyes glittered, but she couldn't be careful. She needed to know.

Or maybe she needed *him* to know. To face up to whatever ghosts seemed to haunt him.

'Are you going to claim it was pure coincidence that he was there when you were, Nikhil?'

'Perhaps it was.'

He looked furious. Again. But, whether he liked what she had to say or not, he was still answering her. That had to stand for something. She couldn't stop now.

'On your birthday?' she countered. 'I think not. I think he cares more than you are willing to admit.'

'You're wrong.'

'Maybe I am,' she acknowledged, 'because how would I know? You said you'd "lost" him a long time ago but you made it sound like he had died. And don't pretend it was my interpretation, because we both know the truth. So, whatever happened between you, the fact is that he was there in Chile, on your birthday, waiting to see you. So is it at all possible, if you stop being defensive and just *think* for a moment, that maybe I'm seeing something you aren't?'

Isla had no idea how, or why, she had the courage to argue with him. It was as though that moment—that expression when he'd first seen the knife—had been her first glimpse of Nikhil. A flash of the real man who lay behind that front he so artfully presented to the world.

And now she'd seen that brief glimpse she couldn't let it go. She wanted more of it. More of him.

'You don't understand,' he growled.

'I'm sure that's true.' It was incredible how her voice sounded so even, betraying none of the churning, swirling emotions she felt inside.

Not even a tremor.

'You push and push, Isla.' He spoke so quietly then, it was almost dangerous. 'What is it that you hope to gain?'

And even though her skin goosebumped in response, even though her heart suddenly accelerated and galloped, thundering as loudly and as heavily as hoofbeats, she held her ground.

Surely it should terrify her that it mattered so much to her?'

'I want to understand you better, Nikhil.'

'Why?' he demanded, his voice harsh, uncompromising.

And still it didn't deter her.

She tilted her head to one side, her stomach feeling as though it had crept up her windpipe and was now lodged somewhere in her throat. She would never know how she managed to sound so calm.

'Why not? Tell me, Nikhil, or so help me, I'll walk out of that door.'

CHAPTER ELEVEN

HE SHOULD LET her go, of course. It would solve all of his problems.

Except for the biggest one of all, that was. Namely, that he couldn't bear the thought of her actually leaving. What was it about this woman that got under his skin? There she was, creeping around his head—no, *striding* around it— and kicking open doors he'd long thought locked and barred.

Even now she stared at him, her head cocked as though she had every right to ask the questions she was asking.

The worrying part was that, as much as he resented the intrusion, he couldn't bring himself to walk away from her. As though a part of him *wanted* to hear what she had to say. Worse, as though a part of him wanted to answer those questions that were falling from her lips.

So why not? What better way to show her the monster that you are?

The voice was almost insidious, and even as

Nikhil tried to silence it, he couldn't. It taunted him, telling him that if she knew the truth about him then she'd surely run as fast and as far as she could in the opposite direction.

And wasn't that what he claimed to want?

'Fine.' He gritted his teeth at last. 'You want to know me, then don't say that I didn't warn you.'

But, instead of looking apprehensive, as he'd expected, she cast him an almost scornful look.

'Is this you playing the role of *Big Bad Nikhil*? Only I have to tell you I've seen it before, and it doesn't convince me.'

'It should.' He resisted the urge to step closer to her. *Barely.* 'But if you really need more convincing, then allow me to indulge you.'

With a supreme effort he made himself step back. Away.

'The day Daksh was in Chile, he *was* there to see me. Though the fact that it was my birthday is almost certainly pure coincidence. Either way, it would have been the first time we'd seen each other since I was fifteen. Since the day of our father's funeral.'

Almost two decades later—it still rankled. More than rankled, if he were to be honest. Good thing he'd learned to be so adept at lying to himself, then.

'What did he want?' Isla asked, when he didn't continue.

'I don't know,' he answered. 'Neither do I care.'

'I think that's a lie.'

Her voice was soft, so soft that it almost felt like a caress, and yet it was almost his undoing that she seemed to read him as easily as she did.

'That I know, or that I care?' he demanded, more to buy himself time than anything else.

'I think you care more than you want to admit.'

He chose not to answer. Instead he clung onto that old, familiar rage that had started to recede from him ever since she'd walked into his life. But he wasn't fooled. He wouldn't be stupid enough to think that it had suddenly disappeared after all these years.

All that anger, and resentment, and grief. All that debilitating guilt. This unique, incredible woman might have unwittingly chased it off for a moment, but it had to have gone somewhere.

It would only stay away for so long—until the novelty of someone as different as her wore off. Then it would be back, as dark, and winding, and bleak as ever.

Which was why he couldn't let her get close to him. He couldn't risk taking her down with him, when he eventually fell.

However hard it was—however much he'd kept

this story inside and not told a single soul for almost twenty years—he had to say it now. He had to find a way to say all those ugly, twisted, damning words.

And the easiest way was to do it quickly. Like ripping off a plaster.

'My brother left me to rot in the home of our drunk, violent, abusive father.'

'Your father hurt you?'

She looked shocked for a split second, and then caught herself, slipping back that doctor's mask of hers.

He told himself there was no need to hate it.

'To be fair, our mother bore the brunt of his alcohol-induced temper when Daksh and I were growing up. But when she died, he found a new punchbag in Daksh.'

'Did he…hit you both?'

'Daksh protected me. He was twelve and I was ten. I guess he thought it was his duty as the big brother.' Nikhil lifted his shoulders, forcing down that bubbling thing inside him that he feared was too much like emotion.

'For four years, he took the beatings when the old man didn't have enough money for his boozing—which went from near the end of the month, to halfway through the month, to every day by the end. Daksh was earning money by then—

we both were, but he was bringing in the main money for the house—and our father took every penny of it he could get his hands on.'

'For his drinking.' Isla spoke quietly, her way of encouraging him on, he knew.

Nikhil tilted his head, the bitterness tasting acrid in his throat.

'Then one day Daksh got offered a couple of months on a fishing vessel. It was a way out, and he took it.'

'Leaving you behind to face your father alone?'

'And the loss of the main source of income,' he ground out. 'He was furious. I was battered black and blue, hit with his leather belt—usually the buckle end—and knocked out more times than I can remember that first month. Then he realised I could take over my errant brother's old job and bring in more money, so he laid off me for a while.'

'The night I turned fifteen, I went out for a celebratory drink with some of the other fishermen—as far as they were concerned I was a working man not a kid, so they gave me little choice. It was just the one drink, and they bought it for me, but my father was in there, and to him I was spending *his* drinking money.'

'He beat you, didn't he?'

She tried not to react, but he heard it nonetheless, and it was oddly soothing, the fact that this beautiful, vivacious woman had had stepfather after stepfather and never once suffered anything like it.

It also said more for Isla's mother than he cared to acknowledge. Perhaps it wouldn't have hurt him to have been a little less abrasive towards her.

'The old man didn't say anything in the pub, but that night he rolled in, barely able to stand he was so blind drunk, and the belt came off.'

'Didn't you stop him?'

'No, I took it. It was easier to take it. It would be over quicker that way. But that night he didn't stop.' Nikhil blocked out the memory, forcing himself to just say the words, not to actually *feel* them. 'The next thing I knew, he'd stumbled to the kitchen and grabbed a knife.'

Her hand moved to her throat and he heard the stifled sound. And what did it mean that a huge part of him wanted to cross that floor and comfort her?

'Your scar...' The anguish in her voice made him feel far too good. Not because of her pain, of course. More at the fact that she evidently cared.

When was the last time anyone had ever cared for him like that? Daksh, before he'd left all those years ago. His mother before that. But otherwise…there was no one.

'He was standing there, waving it around, swaying,' Nikhil remembered. 'I thought he didn't have the strength—or the ability to move in a straight line—to actually do anything about it.'

He let out a bark of laughter that didn't hold a hint of humour in it.

'Suddenly, he rushed me. I couldn't get out of the way fast enough, and the next thing I knew I was flying backwards and he had me pinned to the wall. Then he lifted the knife and drove it through my shoulder.'

He remembered that look on his father's face. The hateful, smug look of triumph as he'd laughed at Nikhil, pinned to the wall with the knife, unable to move. The threat to leave him there whilst he went to pick up his belt. The fear that once his father started he wouldn't stop, and Nikhil wouldn't be able to move, or run. Not that he was about to tell Isla that. It was too brutal, and he didn't want to subject her to it.

'I grabbed the knife, I don't know how, and I somehow yanked it out.'

He stopped as her expression changed. And he hated the way she looked at him in that moment.

The horror, the anguish, but also, far worse than any of that, the flash of fear.

'Nikhil…you said the last time you saw your brother was at your father's funeral…when you were fifteen?'

'You wanted to know what kind of a man I am.' He threw his hands up. 'Now you know. I'm not a man at all. I'm the monster people talk about, write about.'

'Nikhil, what happened?'

'You don't need me to say the words, *pyar*.' He laughed again, but this sound was even worse. He'd called her *pyar*. *My love*. Where had that come from? 'You already know.'

'I don't.' She shook her head. 'I can't believe that. You're…*you*.'

'And I'm a monster. And that's all you need to know. You asked for the truth. I gave it to you. You can't change it now just because you don't like it.'

And even though he'd known what he was all these years, it sounded so horrific falling from his lips in this room, with Isla standing across from him.

He suddenly realised he'd have done anything not to be the kind of man who'd put that expression on her beautiful face.

She stared at him a moment longer, then shook her head.

'It was self-defence, surely? How did it happen? Nikhil, please talk to me.'

'To what end?' He felt as though the words were being torn from his lips. 'What more do you want me to tell you?'

'I want you to talk me through it.'

'No.'

'Please, Nikhil,' she cried. 'You've told me this much. What have you got to lose?'

'It was the worst night of my life. You think I want to relive it?'

'I think you're afraid to.'

And it was the way she stared at him, unblinking, and so confident in him, that was his undoing. It made him wish for things that could never be. And that was the most hollow, scraping feeling of all. He stared at her, his mind in tumult.

'Even if I wanted to, I don't remember anything after pulling the knife out of my shoulder,' he ground out at last. 'It's all hazy.'

'What about the police? Surely they were called?'

'Yes.'

'Then what did they say?'

She clearly wasn't going to let it go. He could tell her what she wanted to hear—so easily—but that didn't mean he believed it. A fresh shame threatened to overwhelm him.

'The police exonerated me,' he offered flatly. 'Apparently there was a neighbour who told them what my father was. She'd seen it over the years, but she'd been too afraid to ever say anything. When she knew he was dead, she confessed every fight and every beating she'd heard over the years.'

Isla made a sound that was half a cry and half a shout. He made himself continue.

'When the police wrote their report they simply stated that I had passed out through blood loss, that I would have lacked the strength and so my father must have rushed me, and impaled himself on the knife.'

'So then, you did nothing,' she exclaimed.

'I don't believe it.' He shook his head. 'If I did nothing, then why can't I remember it? Why have I blocked it out?'

He didn't realise she'd closed the gap between them until he felt her hands cupping his face tightly, her expression fierce.

'Because you were suffering from blood loss. You said it yourself.'

'It just feels too…convenient,' he growled. 'I'm a monster, *pyar*.'

There was that word again. That term of endearment. Suggesting things that could never be his. He wanted her far too much, even now. *Especially now.* It had to stop.

'I'm a savage, Little Doc. An animal. I always was. He didn't just rush me; it doesn't make sense. I remember that final expression on his face. It was me, Isla. It had to be me. Everything else is just too…easy.'

Her heart felt as though it was breaking inside her very chest. For Nikhil.

She could have just taken him into her arms and made it all okay, Isla realised in that instant. He wanted it—*her*—she could tell. She could read that hunger in his eyes, and it echoed within her.

But that was just sex. He might want it, but he didn't need that. Not just yet. He needed something else entirely.

Shoving aside her own desire for him, as well as every shred of grief she felt on his behalf, she steeled her voice and glowered at him.

'You're an idiot, Nikhil Dara.'

His head jerked up, but she couldn't relent now. She had to stand her ground.

'This isn't about what you remember; this is about the fact that you always have to be in control.'

He frowned. 'I'm second in command of a floating city. It's my job to be in control.'

'And you always do that too,' she made herself snap out.

His voice might as well have been laden with ice. It was so cold. And hard.

'I beg your pardon?'

'You use your job, your career, as a convenient excuse.' Still, she had to remain unmoved. 'But I don't just mean in control of your professional life. I mean in control of *everything*. Even the night we slept together, you still had that hint of restraint. It has just taken me until now to recognise it for what it was.'

'You're reading too much into too little,' he ground out.

But this time she refused to be deterred.

'I don't think that I am. That's what you do, Nikhil. You're taking on the guilt of killing your father because a part of you would rather that than admit that you had no control in that situation. Everything with you is about control. You hold it around you like a shroud. Like armour.'

There was a beat of silence. Long. Promising.

'You're wrong.' Abruptly, Nikhil jerked his head out of her hands and took a step away. 'I'm going for a shower. I suggest that, when I come out, you aren't here.'

She watched him stalk across the room; every long, edgy line of his magnificent body was taut with suppressed emotion.

Her mind turned over for several long minutes after he'd closed that bathroom door behind him. But, far from feeling pushed aside, his actions had only underscored how right she was about him.

She could hear the sound of the shower running, a sign of Nikhil trying to claw his way back to normality. But Isla knew, even if he himself didn't realise it, it was too late for him to regain control. She'd already read the maelstrom of emotions in those rich cocoa depths of his eyes. She was so, so close to reaching the real Nikhil.

Slowly at first, then gaining confidence with every step, she crossed the room and slipped into the bathroom, letting the door click loudly behind her.

'What are you doing, Little Doc?' Raw emotion sliced through his words, his eyes darkening as he watched her.

'I'm not wrong,' she said. Softly this time. 'You wear so much armour that it's practically suffocating you, and you don't even know it.'

And if she wanted to pierce it—if she wanted

to reach him—then she was going to have to create a weak spot.

Slowly, she unbuttoned her shirt and let it fall to the floor, and he swallowed but didn't speak. His jaw locked, a tiny pulse betraying his otherwise still appearance.

The rest of her clothing followed. Then she stepped into the large cubicle with him.

'I'll ask again.' His ragged breathing bolstered her confidence all the more. 'What are you doing? Is it that you won't answer, Little Doc? Or that you *can't*?'

She cocked her head on one side, her eyes meeting his boldly.

'I thought you used to call me that nickname to be sweet. Now I realise it's your way of reminding yourself of my job; reminding yourself to keep your distance; reminding yourself to stay in control.'

'I don't need nicknames to stay in control.'

She didn't answer. Not at first. She merely took a pace forward, as if silently matching him. And now they were so close that if he'd lifted his arm up he could have touched her. He *wanted* to touch her; she knew him well enough by now to tell.

'Getting you to relinquish control. Just for once,' she told him at last.

'Is that so?' he demanded through gritted teeth.

Isla made herself smile. 'It is.'

Then, reaching up onto her tiptoes, as the waterfall shower cascaded over them both, she pressed her lips to his.

CHAPTER TWELVE

HAD HE BEEN waiting a whole lifetime just to kiss her again?

It felt like it. And that mere realisation should have made him take stock. Instead it walloped into him, winding him, before turning infinitely softer and moving like a caress over him. It was a smile that made him take another—possibly perilous—step closer.

As though he was compelled.

He struggled, trying to pull together some semblance of discipline. Though whether for her or for himself he couldn't be sure. He'd spent his whole adult life feeling as though there was a monster prowling deep inside him, lurking in the dark, stalking around the edges. He'd thought of himself as some kind of ringmaster, trying to keep that monster in check.

Now, abruptly, he felt as though he wasn't the one with the power at all. She was—*Isla was*—and she was leading him by the nose.

Or something rather further down.

As if she was weaving some kind of magic around him, binding him. Worse, he *liked* it.

'Whatever game you think you're playing, Isla,' he ground out, only just able to pull his mouth from hers, 'it won't work.'

'And if I'm not playing a game?'

The suggestiveness in her words licked over him, blood pooling in the very hardest part of him. It was too much to think she wouldn't notice, when her eyes slid lower and widened that fraction.

Aside from the running water, the silence was hot, and heavy. Pulling around him, closing in until he felt it pressing on his lungs and stopping him from breathing properly.

And then, *God help him*, she licked her lips.

Nikhil didn't remember reaching out. He didn't remember hauling her to him. But suddenly she was there, in his arms, and he was kissing her as though he was a suffocating man and she was the oxygen he needed to survive.

Perhaps she was.

He'd certainly never felt so desperate, so ferocious, so feral before. He slid his tongue against hers, revelling in the way she met him stroke for stroke. The way she took his lip in her teeth and grazed it with just enough pressure.

Need fired through him. Raw. Unrestrained. It

made the beast inside him roar. He would have her screaming his name again, as she had that first night.

Even the memory of it was intensified, now that he had her in his arms. It took everything he had not to simply lift her in his arms, carry her to the bed and rip her clothes off so he could indulge in every last erotic fantasy he'd had about her.

'I told you.' She drew back unexpectedly, as if reading his mind. 'Tonight isn't about me losing control.'

He wasn't prepared for the sense of loss, especially when desire was still unmistakable in her tone, her dark, lust-filled eyes never leaving his.

He wanted to pull her back to him. He didn't know how he resisted. Maybe because that male part of him still wanted to make her come back to him. To beg him.

'Then what?' he bit out; for the first time in a couple of decades he wasn't sure he trusted himself.

Every second of silence wrapped tighter around him. He felt more and more wired. And somehow Isla knew it. More than knew it—she was relishing it.

And just when he thought she wasn't going to speak, she stretched her hand out and ran it straight down the length of his body. Over his chest, his belly, her eyes never leaving his. Then, slowly and deliberately, she wrapped her hand around him, one long, elegant finger at a time, sliding from root to tip, leaving him forgetting to even breathe.

'Isla…' he warned. Weakly, if he was to be truthful.

'Like I said, I didn't come here to lose control.' He drew in a sharp breath at the sudden wicked glint in her eyes as, without warning, she sank elegantly to her knees in front of him. 'I came here this time so *you* would lose control.'

In that instant Nikhil knew he needed to stop her. He'd had countless women pleasure him this way, over the years, and he'd welcomed it. Encouraged it. Sometimes downright instigated it. But this was the first time he had ever, *ever,* felt like this. As though she was asking him to surrender to her. And he couldn't do that.

Then, that devilish gaze still locked with his, she leaned forward and took him straight into her mouth. And as his legs turned to water right there and then, Nikhil found he was powerless to do anything but let her do what she willed, whilst he thought he was about to die from need.

Pleasuring Nikhil was possibly the most sensuous thing she'd ever done in her life, Isla thought.

Oh, she'd performed the act before, but it had never, *ever* felt so heady. So right. It had never made her feel as powerful as she did right now, with him.

As though she had all the control and he was simply at her mercy.

With every stroke of her tongue, every tightening of her fist, every graze of her teeth, she could hear his breathing grow all the more ragged and those hewn stone thighs of his tremble that little bit harder.

She drew him out to let her tongue swirl around his velvet-steel tip, then angled her head to take him in deeper. Her mouth, her tongue, her hands, all working in harmony, united in the same goal of making Nikhil give himself up to her completely.

And his taste. It was intoxicating. Stirring. It made her want to indulge all the more. Indulge for ever.

She was in so much trouble and she couldn't seem to care.

The realisation dragged a low moan from deep in her throat, rumbling down Nikhil's length and eliciting a curse from him as he speared his fingers deeper into her hair. As if he couldn't help himself. Another shiver of excitement jolted through Isla.

Gripping him tighter, she let her fingers apply pressure at his root whilst her mouth worked some kind of spell she hadn't even known she possessed. Until Nikhil's breath came harsher, his legs less stable than ever. She was driving him closer and closer to the edge and the taste of victory, of power, was almost too delicious.

And still she wasn't surprised when he found that last shred of strength to pull away from her.

'Not like this.' His voice was so thick, so gravelly, that it was almost unrecognisable.

It gave her an immense sense of satisfaction—almost making up for the sense of loss.

Then he was slamming off the shower, gathering her into his arms and carrying her back into the bedroom as if he couldn't contain himself any longer.

He threw her down on the bed, stared at her for a long moment before offering a guttural sound of approval that juddered straight through her, and threw her legs over his shoulders. Then he licked into her greedily, urgently, without a single word spoken.

Bright and hot, like the sunlight bouncing off the waves outside her window every morning.

Better.

Isla wasn't sure how she didn't shatter in an instant. Because he didn't merely lick her, he feasted on her. As if she was the last meal of his life and he was hell-bent on sampling every last morsel. And she was helpless to do anything but spread herself out for him, every sweep of his tongue making her shake that little bit more uncontrollably, her hands thrust into his hair, her hips bucking up to meet him.

She felt utterly wanton. And somehow she knew that only fired Nikhil up all the more. She was hurtling to the edge and there was no way she could apply the brakes, especially when he cupped her backside with his large hands, pressed down on her sex with his mouth and then sucked. Hard.

Isla fractured apart, his name tumbling from her lips—a song and an incantation. She splintered, and still he kept going, relentlessly pushing her from one high to the next. She arched her back, her fingers grasping his hair, his shoulders, the sheets, for some kind of purchase, and his low rumble of laughter shuddered through her like a new form of exquisite, magnificent torture.

And this time she didn't simply hit another high; this time she hurtled off into space. And she could only hope that Nikhil would be her safety net when she fell back down to earth.

Isla had no idea how long it took her to come back to herself, but when she did she glanced around the room to check where she was. To make sure that it hadn't just been a dream.

But it hadn't. She was still here, in his room, and in his bed. She just didn't understand how he could upend her world like this—so easily—and yet the room wasn't equally torn apart.

Then he was moving up her body to cover it with his own as she reached for him, nestling him between her legs. A low gasp escaped her lips as she rolled her hips against him, revelling in the way his breath caught, the way they affected each other with barely a brush of heat against steel.

But wasn't this supposed to be about her being in control? She had almost forgotten. Lifting her hands to his shoulders, Isla made a supreme effort and pushed him off her, onto his back on the bed, straddling him before he could move.

Nikhil's expression flip-flopped between lust and amusement. 'Like that, is it?'

'Like that,' she whispered, leaning forward to brush her mouth to his, her tongue teasing at the seam of his lips.

Her chest pressed to his, her nipples chafing deliciously against the fine layer of hair scattered across his chest. She was so close. Again. How could that be?

His hands splayed around her hips. Lightly. As

if he was trying to resist taking the reins—but only just. She liked that he even tried. Her gaze caught his and, for another moment, she couldn't breathe. Placing her hands on his shoulders, Isla levered herself slightly upright and, her eyes still locked with his, she slipped slowly—so slowly—down his length, taking him inside her.

Deep, and sure.

It was possibly the most provocative thing she'd ever done. And Nikhil seemed to think so too. His jaw was so tight she was half afraid he might break it.

'See what happens when you give up control?' she whispered, her eyes still held by his. 'Even for this tiny moment.'

'I only know that you're killing me, *pyar*,' he ground out.

And suddenly his perpetually dark expression cleared, if only for a moment, and she saw something in those depths that she had never anticipated. Something that called to her so loudly, and so clearly. A jagged puzzle piece, like those pieces of jewellery that were two halves of a whole. And, not that she'd ever realised it before, the matching piece lay—just as deeply buried—inside her.

It called to her, clawed at her and, even if she couldn't bring herself to answer, there was no way she could stop her heart from swelling in her chest. Insane, and dangerous, and just as undeniable.

And then she wasn't in control any longer. Nikhil's hands tightened around her hips and he began to set the pace. Slow yet inexorable, beating in her chest, her belly, and through her very veins. Building deliciously and carrying her higher still as her fingers bit into his shoulders as she matched him, thrust for thrust.

'Nikhil...'

'Forget about control, *pyar*,' he muttered, his voice gratifyingly strained. 'Forget about everything and just let go.'

'You first,' she murmured, scarcely recognising her own voice.

Her entire body was fizzing as she began to move again, riding them both towards the edge. And suddenly it didn't matter who had fallen first as they toppled together, over the edge and into the gloriously endless abyss beyond.

It was an hour or so later when Isla swung her legs heavily over the side of the bed as Nikhil lay sleeping. She ached everywhere. A delicious bone-deep ache that reminded her of every last second of that glorious time together.

An ache that made her hesitate as her feet made contact with the wooden floor, wishing she didn't have to force herself to get up. To sneak out.

It was supposed to have been about quenching her thirst for Nikhil. How could it be that, instead, the more she had of this man, the more she seemed to crave?

Well, either way, it was too bad. They'd had their indulgence; he wasn't going to welcome her still being around when he woke. Nikhil would be about business, the way he was always about business. But this afternoon had been something special. Just between them. A moment where he had relaxed his control…and a memory she would have for ever…where Nikhil had been at her mercy—if only for a few hours.

She tucked it away as something precious.

Leaning forward a fraction, Isla placed her fists either side of her bottom, pushing into the mattress, and levered her reluctant body up.

'Going somewhere?'

She swung around quickly.

God, he still looked so impossibly beautiful. It wasn't fair, really.

'It's nearly dinnertime. I thought I should get changed for the evening.'

He frowned. 'You don't have to do that.'

Her heart faltered in her chest. Could he possibly want her to stay? Her blood pumped harder in her veins and she tried to quell it. Even if he did want her to stay, she shouldn't. It was already starting to become too difficult to separate the sex from the emotion.

'I'm the scheduled doctor on call,' she offered instead, chewing on her lower lip, almost frightened of saying too much and spooking him.

'You have your pager?'

'Of course.' She looked around for her clothes, flushing when she saw them lying haphazardly on the floor, and remembering Nikhil's impatience at removing them.

The moment had been intoxicating. The memory still was, if she were to be honest. And yet she swept up the garments and held them to the front of her body, as though that provided her with any more dignity than standing here, completely naked, in front of him.

'Then they can reach you if they need to. You don't have to be down there with everyone else.'

'Right.' Isla swallowed.

She could barely breathe right now. Standing here, waiting—silently begging—for him to spell it out. But Nikhil just lay there, his hands locked behind his head, his bare muscled chest on display and the white sheet low over his abdomen, just concealing himself from her.

Teasing her.

Was he daring her to crawl back onto the bed and repeat what had happened earlier?

Her mouth actually watered, even as insecurity gripped her.

'So... I should stay?'

His eyes changed, something flashing through them that she couldn't quite identify, and then they darkened, looking more sensuous than ever.

'Are you waiting for an invitation?'

What was it about his tone that made her suddenly so bold?

'I wasn't presuming,' she teased. 'I've learned that can be a mistake where you are concerned.'

'And I've learned that no matter how much I try to resist you, *pyar*, I cannot. But there is a lesson to be learned there, I think.'

'What lesson?' Isla asked, trying to hold herself together. Trying not to read too much into the fact that he'd called her *pyar*. Again. Which, if she wasn't very much mistaken, was a term of endearment.

It was both terrifying and stirring that she should react so viscerally to the term. No matter how much she kept trying to remind herself that this was casual, that it didn't mean anything, that she didn't *want* it to mean anything, Isla was very much afraid her head and her heart weren't quite singing the same song.

Perhaps reading that all over her face, Nikhil suddenly took hold of her upper arms. Not roughly, but enough to make sure she was listening to him.

'Isla, you understand that I can't offer you anything more than this?' His voice was gruff.

'I don't want anything more.' The words slipped out easily enough. Yet she was still suspicious of her own traitorous heart. 'You forget, I don't believe in love. Or relationships.'

'So you said,' he confirmed.

But he didn't look entirely convinced and she knew how he felt.

'The point is, this isn't dating. It's just…'

'Enjoying each other's company,' Isla jumped in, though whether she was trying to convince Nikhil or herself wasn't entirely determinable.

Still, the words were the right ones. And, whether he believed her or not, it was enough to allow him to continue.

'Enjoying each other's company,' he muttered, already pulling her back to him and claiming her mouth with his own. As if he couldn't help himself any longer.

And didn't that say something all of its own?

CHAPTER THIRTEEN

WHAT WAS IT about an all-you-can-eat cruise ship buffet that induced a passenger with a known allergy to decide to sample the very food that could kill them? In this case, a newly married fifty-year-old gentleman with a shellfish allergy who had nonetheless decided to sample the aphrodisiac qualities of oysters with his new wife.

In a way, she could almost understand it. The past few weeks with Nikhil—ever since that night back at the hotel in the rainforest—had been incredible. Special. How many times had he reached for her that night? After that thrilling moment when she'd been about to sneak out of his room, when he'd told her that he couldn't offer her anything more than enjoying each other's company.

It had been more of a promise than she'd ever imagined she would hear from his lips. And he'd made good on it, giving her the key to his cabin every night they happened to be off together. Trusting her.

Because, as discreet as she'd tried to be, she knew that even if only one person spotted them, it would ruin the reputation he'd spent a decade building. He was risking it for her. It was more of a declaration to her than all the words he'd avoided saying. And one day, when she had the courage, maybe she could point that out to him and prove that he was wrong for thinking that he wasn't the kind of person who could love, or be loved.

Maybe. One day.

And Nikhil wasn't the only one who had changed this past month. How many times had she caught herself thinking and feeling differently? How many times had she felt wild, and daring, just because of the way this one, wonderful man affected her?

She was growing; she could sense it. She just wasn't quite sure what it meant yet.

But, either way, perhaps it wasn't such a shock that the new marriage made her latest patient feel as though he was invincible—even where shellfish were concerned. Taking the stairs two at a time, she raced to the main restaurant. Hopefully, he would have his allergy pen on him and his new wife would have administered it.

She might have known it wouldn't happen. Even by the time she'd elbowed her way through the rubber-necking crowd, the patient was deteriorating rapidly. His face had swollen up at least twice its usual size, contorted and red, and threatening his airway with every passing second. His breathing was already shallow and rasping, and even the guy's hands were swollen where he'd picked up the offending item.

His wife was evidently so distraught that it took Isla several moments to calm her down enough to discover that her husband's name was Stewart.

Clearing a space around her patient, Isla picked out an epinephrine injector from her bag and prepared to administer the medication, talking to where the eyes should have been on Stewart's distorted face. She was only glad that it was a lunchtime and the man was wearing shorts.

It was fortunate that, just as she finished, Lisa arrived with antihistamines and an oxygen mask, the mobile gurney not far behind.

'Let's get you to the medical centre, Stewart.' Isla smiled at her patient, wondering if he could even see her. He seemed to be able to, but it was still too hard to tell. This was always the worst part, trying to deal with a frightened patient and equally frightened loved one when a hundred or more people were crowding around, trying to get a good view of the action.

It was several hours before Isla finally finished up the last of her paperwork, handed it to Gerd, who was on duty for the night, and slipped out of the medical centre.

Quickly and quietly, she hurried through the ship, grateful for the late hour if only because it made it easier to sneak to Nikhil's room without being seen. Not that the past couple of weeks hadn't been just a little bit thrilling, sneaking around the ship, snatching as many precious nights together as they could without anyone realising what was going on.

Not that they got that many between his work and hers, but in a way that only made them feel that much more delicious.

Some feat on a ship like this, and for Isla, who'd never done anything remotely illicit like this before, it was impossible not to get a bit of a kick from it.

No doubt it helped that the only two people who might possibly notice that something was amiss were either in some secret location with the other Dara brother...or holed up with the Captain on his downtime.

Ironic, really. Isla stifled a gurgle of laugher.

She had slipped inside Nikhil's cabin when he was there, and he was drawing her into his arms and to him.

'I wasn't sure if you'd still be on the bridge,' she breathed between scorching, devilish kisses.

'I got back here a few minutes before you did,' he muttered. 'I heard about the drama with the seafood roulette player. He's okay?'

'He's okay,' she confirmed, her fingers making their way to his waist to tug his already half-undone shirt out of the trouser band.

'Anything I need to know?'

'Nothing that can't wait for the report in the morning,' she said, shaking her head.

'Good,' he approved, pulling her up to wrap her legs around his waist and carry her across the room to drop her—both of them laughing like intoxicated teens on their first night out—onto the bed.

Isla was just finishing in the shower an hour or so later when she heard a soft knock on Nikhil's cabin door and the low exchange of voices. She paused, trying to stay quiet and discreet and not really trying to listen. Not that it mattered; the voices were too low for her to hear what was being said.

Waiting for the sound of the door closing, Isla wrapped the towel around herself and stepped out of the bathroom. She schooled herself to stay silent, torn between the fact that this was Nikhil's cabin and it was therefore likely to be ship's business, and sheer curiosity over what such a late-night call had been about.

But when she rounded the corner to see Nikhil standing, his face a shade of white to match the towel slung loosely around his hips, she didn't stop to think.

'What's wrong, Nikhil? What's happened?'

His eyes slid to her, but she had the strangest impression that he wasn't really seeing her. A moment later, he seemed to refocus.

'It's nothing.'.

'It doesn't look like nothing,' she pressed softly. In truth, he looked tormented. Defeated. And she could feel her insides twist themselves in knots as she fought the urge to go to him and try to make everything all right. Because she knew she couldn't.

She wasn't his girlfriend; she was…little more than a booty call. A supposedly mutually agreeable booty call, but suddenly she wondered if her mother had truly been right all these years.

Had her marriages always been mutually advantageous, or was it possible that they had been more one-sided than Marianna had ever realised? Or indeed admitted. Could it be that the husbands Marianna had selected had each fallen a little bit in love with her, in their own way?

Nikhil had warned her that he couldn't offer her anything more than *enjoying each other's company,* and she had agreed on the premise that she'd never wanted to get hurt again after Bradley.

But really, deep down, Isla was beginning to finally admit a truth she suspected she'd known all along. She had never loved Bradley; she'd barely felt much for him at all, so how could he ever have hurt her?

Had the emotions she'd held up as evidence of her hurt really been more about humiliation? Because she'd felt more for Nikhil in the last few weeks than she ever had for her ex-fiancé. Which made her fear that her affair with Nikhil wasn't quite so emotion-free as she'd imagined.

Certainly not as emotion-free as Nikhil.

But then, instead of shutting her out as she'd expected him to do, Nikhil suddenly picked up an exquisitely written note and passed it to her.

'That was Roberto at the door,' he told her woodenly, referring to the concierge. 'He just delivered this.'

It was such an unexpected invitation into his personal life, yet Isla wasn't about to back away now. Her fingers shaking, she read the message. It was short and to the point and as she came to the end it was impossible to name what skittered through her.

'Your brother wants to meet again?' she stated redundantly.

'At any of the next ports of call.' Nikhil didn't even sound like himself. 'If I name it, he claims he'll be there.'

'Maybe you should,' she offered tentatively. 'Maybe it's time to find out what he wants.'

'Maybe I don't care what he wants,' Nikhil threw back, but she knew he wasn't angry at her.

'Then think about what you want,' she tried instead. 'Or, more pertinently, what you need.'

'I don't need him,' Nikhil bit out flatly, staring at her so hard that she felt his gaze was actually imprinting itself on her skin. 'I might have, a few decades ago. But I don't any more.'

'What happened, Nikhil?'

He shook his head. 'It's long-buried history. I see no benefit in resurrecting it.'

'And yet you chose to tell me about this, when you could have ignored it, as you did the last time he was in touch.'

Nikhil didn't answer, yet she could feel his emotions circling the room. Snaking around them, ready to strike. She knew she ought to keep out of it, but she couldn't. He needed her, whether he recognised it or not.

'What's your history with your brother, Nikhil?'

That pulse ticked harder, faster in his jaw, but he still didn't answer. And then, just as she was about to give up, he opened his mouth.

'He betrayed me, Isla. He was my big brother, and he left me at the very moment that I needed him most. That's all you need to know.'

'Really, Nikhil?' The words spilled from her lips before she could stop them. 'You think you're the only one to have been betrayed by someone? People do that. It's one of the uglier sides to human nature. But you want to know what one of our better qualities is?'

'I'm sure you're going to enlighten me.'

'We pick ourselves up—' she didn't let his wry tone derail her '—dust ourselves off, and we start again.'

'And who, might I ask, betrayed you? Your loving mother? Your idolising stepsister?'

And she didn't know what made her say it; she only knew she wanted to make a point to Nikhil.

'Try my lying ex-fiancé.'

Nikhil bit back whatever response he might have made. He'd spent the better part of a month trying to deny it, but the question of Isla's ex-fiancé had plagued him ever since he'd seen that light band around her ring finger.

From that very first day it had begged the question of what kind of man let a woman like Isla Sinclair slip through his fingers. And that was why, from that very first day, he'd realised quite how much trouble he was in when it came to this remarkable, bewitching woman.

'I met Bradley at med school, and I was with him for ten years. The last three of those years we were engaged.'

'Let me guess; he cheated on you.'

'He did.' She nodded. 'Many times, I discovered that final week before we broke up. But do you want to know the sickest part? That wasn't even the thing that hurt me the most.'

'Is that so?' he managed, fighting not to let her see the unexpected anger which had begun to swell inside him at her admission.

Indignation on Isla's behalf. A desire to find this idiot *Bradley* and show him how duplicitous cowards like him deserved to be treated. But, more than that, Nikhil had to fight a sense that Isla deserved more, *better,* than to be cheated on.

Just as she deserves more than being used as a booty call? a voice demanded in his head.

'The worst part...' She licked her lips as though she was finding this harder than she'd expected. 'The worst part was that I let him dictate my life. I let him tell me that once we were married I was going to give up my medical career and become the kind of wife that could support *his* career.'

Nikhil blinked. Of all the admissions he'd expected from her, this was not one of them.

Isla was born to be a doctor; she clearly loved her work and she was good at it. It would be like throwing him off a ship and telling him to find a new career on land legs.

'And you agreed to this?'

She tilted her head to one side thoughtfully. 'I didn't disagree. At least, not at first. He was saying all the things that my mother had always wanted, so for a short while I lost myself.'

'I can't imagine that of you.'

'I was, frankly, an idiot. But I thought I loved him. And I thought that he loved me. It turned out he just loved my mother's social contacts. I was little more than a means to an end. Albeit one who also looked good on his arm.'

'I still can't see you being the kind of person who would agree to that.' Nikhil shook his head as Isla squeezed her eyes shut.

'That's the point. I was a different person back then. That moment was the catalyst for me to try to turn my life around. To become a ship's doctor, to tour the world, and to have the career I'd always wanted. I didn't bank on meeting someone like you.'

And though he warned himself not to react, that he shouldn't like the way that sounded, Nikhil found himself carried away by her words.

'I've changed, Nikhil. I'm not the girl I was a month ago. I might not have quite noticed it, but my mother has. And she put it down to you, that night at the gala.'

And God help him, but he wanted to believe every word that she was saying. He just knew that he shouldn't.

He had his own demons. And, unlike Isla, he didn't have the strength to confront them.

'That wasn't the agreement,' he balked. 'We said *no dating*, just enjoying time together. We agreed *no commitments*.'

'And now it has developed,' Isla pointed out evenly.

He might have believed her, had it not been for the slight shake in her hands. He gritted his teeth as he fought to harden his heart—whatever heart he had—against her.

'Not for me.'

He certainly didn't expect her soft, almost regretful response.

'You're lying.'

'Say again?'

'I don't know if you're just lying to me or if you're also lying to yourself, but you've felt something blossoming between us, just as I have.'

'You're mistaken.'

'No, I'm not. And you can growl at me all you want to, Nikhil, but it won't change the facts,' she pressed on, inching her way further and further inside the hollow cavern that was his chest.

Only he had the oddest sensation that she was shining light and warmth into the corners of it as she went.

'I don't do intimacy. Or commitment.'

'You didn't, no,' she agreed. 'But you can't pretend that things haven't changed between us over the last few weeks. You're more open, and compassionate. It isn't a weakness.'

He had a terrible, wonderful feeling that she was right.

But she couldn't be right. Because even if what she said was true, even if he'd started to try to become a different person, the truth was that he couldn't. He was who he was. His past had made sure of that. Pretending to be someone different—the kind of man who deserved a woman like Isla—wasn't going to *make* him different.

It would be like papering over the cracks. His flaws would still be there, hidden temporarily beneath. And when they finally began to show again, when they finally broke through the surface, they would be all the uglier.

But the worst part of it was that he *wanted* to believe her.

So damned much.

A part of him thought this might be love—or the closest thing he could ever get to it.

It felt like giving a kid a detonation device and then stepping back to see what happened. It couldn't end well. If he cared for Isla at all, he wouldn't put them in that position. And if that wasn't a reason to keep his distance...

'You're seeing what you want to see,' he practically snarled at her, as if to remind her—remind them both—of the monster that he truly was.

Instead of cowering, however, his beautiful, powerful Isla merely smiled, making everything inside him begin to shatter.

'I'm acknowledging what you pretend isn't there. I see you for who you really are, Nikhil, and, no matter what you try to tell yourself, I know you're a good man.'

'You haven't listened to anything I've told you,' he roared. 'I'm not a good man, Isla, and, no matter that you want to pretend differently, it won't make it true.'

'You're wrong, Nikhil. You have this one awful image of yourself locked in your brain, I suspect because you think that's what your brother saw when he was at that funeral. But the Nikhil you hold onto isn't the man I have ever seen. Not once. You need to meet Daksh and listen to what he has to say.'

And in that moment he realised he would give anything to be the man that Isla thought he was.

But that wasn't him. She was wrong. And so the only thing he could do was protect her from himself. The only way he knew how.

Snatching up his uniform, he stalked out of the room. He had to go and speak to the Captain now, before he thought better of what he was about to do.

'Lock the door when you leave, Isla,' he managed. 'And don't return.'

CHAPTER FOURTEEN

IT WAS ALMOST a week later, when Isla was in the middle of tending to her latest patient, that she was summoned by the Captain.

'Thank you, Gerd.' She pasted on a bright smile, turning back to her rather glamorously dressed patient, who Isla had initially guessed to be in her mid-to-late sixties, but who had turned out to be a sprightly seventy-four.

Mrs Berridge-Jones had tripped down the last steps of the staircase in the Grand Lobby and been brought to the surgery because she'd been unable to put any weight on her ankle.

'I'm not disembarking,' the woman had declared imperiously. 'I've been waiting two years for this cruise. I refuse to be sent home just because I caught my heel in the hem of my wretched dress on the last step of your perfectly easy-to-see staircase. It would just ruin the entire cruise.'

She'd rolled the *r* of *ruin*, and Isla had seen flashes of her mother in Mrs Berridge-Jones.

Now, Isla helped the older woman swing around on the examination table, taking note of the wince of pain.

'Good news, Mrs Berridge-Jones.' Isla grinned as she presented the images to her patient. 'Your X-ray doesn't show any fractures; I'm confident that you've got a sprained ankle rather than a break, so I can say that I have absolutely no intention of ruining your cruise.'

'Jolly glad to hear it. So you'll patch me up in a jiffy and I can get back to my welcome drink? I'd just ordered a rather decent port.'

'As close to a jiffy as I can,' Isla answered wryly, checking over the foot. 'But it's still swollen and clearly painful, even though the painkillers I have given you are doing their job. There are also clear signs of a reduction of movement, so perhaps you won't be back upstairs in time to enjoy your port this evening.'

Mrs Berridge-Jones cast her a distinctly disdainful glance. 'Oh, just give me a few more pain pills to get me through the next couple of days and I shall be as right as rain.'

'Before you go racing back up there to your port, Mrs Berridge-Jones, I have to tell you that sprains still require care and can be very painful. It involves tearing or stretching the ligaments that help hold your ankle bones together and stabilise your ankle joint.'

'I'm not having a splint for a sprained ankle,' the woman scoffed.

Isla smothered another smile as she adopted her best disapproving doctor voice. 'Self-care is vital, Mrs Berridge-Jones. If you don't look after a sprained ankle you could end up with chronic ankle pain, ankle joint instability, or even arthritis in the ankle joint.'

'Piffle.'

'I want to see it elevated and wrapped before I let you leave here, Mrs Berridge-Jones.'

And although the woman blustered, Isla noted she nonetheless obeyed.

Now, an hour later, Isla found herself hammering on Nikhil's door and practically shouldering him out of the way to step inside, without waiting to be invited, the moment he opened it.

'I've just been summoned by the Captain,' she bit out. 'He offered me a new job.'

It was useless pretending that she wasn't nervous. That her heart wasn't suddenly pounding, or her mouth dust-dry.

'Right.'

She hated that he didn't look surprised. Or concerned. Or anything at all, really.

'The doctor who was originally on this ship wants to resume his post when the new cruise begins.'

'Yes, he retains that right.'

She didn't know what she wanted him to say, but it was more than that.

'So they've offered me a post on another ship. Better than the *Hestia,* but not quite the *Cassiopeia* either.'

'It's a good career move.'

Emotions bubbled up in her chest. She'd told herself she was being paranoid, suspecting Nikhil of being somehow involved. But now, given his reaction, she was beginning to suspect worse.

That perhaps he'd been more than just *involved.* That perhaps he'd been the one to actually instigate it.

'You knew,' she accused, her chest feeling as though it was about to crack.

'The Captain asked my opinion. It seems you've made quite an impression on Dr Turner. He wanted to keep you in favour of the original doctor.'

The truth walloped her hard, winding her.

'So you said I was better to move ships.'

'I merely pointed out that not letting the previous doctor resume his post might open us up to legal challenges. And your role here was only ever stated as temporary.'

'You didn't want me here.' Nausea rose in Isla but she quashed it. 'You told me to transfer, and when I refused you found some other way to get rid of me.'

'You got a promotion,' he corrected. 'To a more prestigious ship than you were meant to have been on in the first instance.'

She supposed she should be grateful at least, that he wasn't choosing to lie to her. At least he had the integrity to tell her the truth. But it didn't make it hurt any less.

'This isn't about my career, Nikhil. At least have the decency to admit that. This is about you not wanting to open up to anyone. And my arrival messing up all your little rules that you have for yourself.'

'I considered what was best for the company. That's my job.'

'And thank God it fits with your personal leanings. You've been trying to push me away ever since I came on board. And you've been hating yourself because you couldn't do it.'

'It has nothing to do with *getting rid* of anybody. It has to do with supporting your transfer to another ship when the doctor you were replacing is returning here anyway.'

'No.' She refused to accept it. 'That's a convenient excuse—because it also happens to fit. But it's a side-effect; it isn't the main reason. It isn't your primary motivator. You endorsed that transfer because it also got me away from you. You have feelings for me; you just aren't prepared to admit them.'

'But I won't transfer,' Isla stated flatly. 'What are you so afraid of, Nikhil?'

He blinked. It was fleeting, but it was there nonetheless, and it told her that her hunch—this odd, alien sense—about him had been right.

Isla felt as though she was splitting in two. One part of her celebrated the fact that she knew this incredible, enigmatic man better than he even knew himself.

And the other part of her… That was terrified at the notion. Because she didn't want to be connected with him—with anyone—again. Not after Bradley.

And yet you never felt you knew Bradley a fraction of the way you feel you know Nikhil, whispered a voice inside her head. *You never wanted to.*

'You misunderstand.' His cold voice dragged her back to the moment. 'I'm not afraid. I'm never afraid.'

* * *

He knew it wasn't true even as the defiant words left his lips.

He was more afraid than he'd ever been in his life. And not least because the way Isla looked at him right at that moment made him feel as though she could read every last dark thought engraved on the cold, hard stone that sat in place of his heart.

'You were afraid the moment that message arrived at your cabin the other night, and instead of keeping it from me, as you would have done a week ago, you handed it to me to read.'

'It was just a message, Isla.'

'We both know it wasn't. You let me into your life and now you're regretting it. This is your way of pushing me away.'

'It's for your own good,' he ground out.

'Because you're a monster?' she asked scornfully, and he loved the way she sounded so fierce. *For him.*

'Because in your head it's somehow your fault that your stupid brother left you to suffer everything alone, and never came back?'

He wanted so much to believe her. He almost did—even though, unlike her, he knew the truth.

'I told you that he came to the funeral?' The words might as well have come out independently of his mouth. Certainly, independently of his brain.

'Your father's funeral, yes.' She dipped her head carefully, after a moment.

'He didn't come to the grave, but he stood by a tree and watched. I saw the disgust in his eyes. Like he thought I should have done better for the old man. The bastard was lucky I even gave him that much.'

'You didn't talk to Daksh?' Isla asked softly.

'No more that he talked to me.' Nikhil inclined his head curtly. 'I looked up one moment and he was there, then when I looked up again he was gone.'

'And that's why you think you are this…monster?'

'It's what I am. Even he could see it.'

'You're not. You're a man. And a good man, at that. But the sad part is that you will never take my word for it. I don't matter enough to you.'

And he wanted to refute it, so fervently. But he couldn't.

'So speak to your brother, Nikhil,' she continued, and he would have given so much to erase that desolation from her voice. 'Whatever he has to say, it can't be any worse than this hell that you've put yourself in.'

Then she kissed him and walked out of the door. Out of his life.

And he tried not to wonder what the hell he'd just done.

So this was what the most exclusive hotel in Rotterdam looked like, Nikhil thought as he glanced around the elegant lobby that practically oozed money.

He could pretend that he wasn't looking for answers that would make him the man Isla deserved. Maybe he should tell himself that he was here because the Captain had pulled him in less than twenty-four hours earlier to tell Nikhil that the promotion he'd been working towards for the better part of a decade was now his for the taking. Captain of his own ship.

But, on both counts, Nikhil knew he'd be lying to himself.

Moreover, he didn't deserve a promotion any more than he deserved her. *Isla*.

These past ten days without her had been hell. His entire ten-week cruise had been a rollercoaster—like being on the swell, far out at sea—but the fun part had only started in that third week when he'd walked into that bar in Chile.

And as he'd walked out of the Captain's office he'd found himself heading to the medical centre—instinctively wanting to share his news with Isla.

Nikhil still wasn't sure how he'd stopped himself. He only remembered standing on the deck, on a mercifully cold, rainy sea day, which meant that only a handful of other, waterproof-clad souls had been out there, braving the bracing air. And he'd finally admitted that Isla had been right that his shattered relationship with his brother had been eating him up inside all these years.

In that instant he'd wondered what he had to lose.

Before he could talk himself out it, he'd hurried back to his cabin, conducted an internet search for DXD Industries and picked up his phone.

And then, suddenly, his brother had been at the end of the phone, and Nikhil knew he'd have recognised that voice in an instant.

He'd even imagined he'd heard Isla's voice in his head, encouraging him, as he'd told his brother that their next port of call was going to be Rotterdam. And now here he was, sitting in the plush hotel lobby and waiting for the man he hadn't seen since they'd both been kids.

And then Nikhil saw him.

There was no doubt that Daksh Dara had money. More than that—wealth. It was in every long line of his body, every expensive stitch of his tailored suit.

The two brothers eyed each other for several long moments—perhaps a lifetime—each on their own side of the room. And Nikhil could practically feel the storm of recrimination at the centre of it, cracking and sparking, as the two of them held their ground. As if neither wanted to be the first to make a move.

Eventually, however, to Nikhil's shock, it was Daksh who began the approach—every long, powerful stride seeming to strike the ground with force—making Nikhil wonder which one of them was actually the stronger, after all.

'Nikhil.' Daksh spoke at last.

'Brother,' he replied, infusing each syllable with as much insult as he possibly could.

'It's been a long time.'

'Since we last talked? Or since we last saw each other?' Nikhil asked icily.

The last thing he expected was a flash of something that looked suspiciously like remorse in Daksh's eyes. It knocked him off-guard.

'I was a coward for not talking to you at...*his* funeral.'

Nikhil couldn't answer. He was too caught up in the way his brother had not only refused to call it *our father's funeral*, but also the hit of repulsion in the way he'd said *his*. As though he couldn't stand the old man any more than Nikhil could.

'I thought it was because you felt he deserved better than I gave him,' he managed stiffly.

And there it was, the look of disgust on his brother's face that Nikhil had seen at the funeral. Nikhil braced himself as Daksh opened his mouth to speak again.

'I didn't think he deserved anything even that good.'

It was about as far from anything Nikhil had been expecting as it could be.

'Say again?'

'He was a monster. I didn't think he even deserved the dignity of a funeral.'

Something coursed through Nikhil at that moment. Thick, and intense, though he couldn't have said what it was.

'Then why the hell didn't you even say one word to me?'

For a long moment Daksh didn't speak, and when he did it wasn't to answer.

'Shall we order a drink?' he asked, though it wasn't really a question.

Then he simply lifted his hand and a suited man moved instantly, one of several discreetly dotted around the room that Nikhil now realised were part of his brother's entourage.

Daksh had an entourage?

They sat in a heavy silence, each silently evaluating the other, until a waiter materialised with two tumblers of rich amber liquid. Its peppery tobacco heat pervaded his nostrils, telling him this was a quality not even seen at the Captain's table.

They both took a pull simultaneously, sending heat and spice across Nikhil's palate, followed by a creaminess that ended in rich, spicy fruits. It was impressive, though he wasn't about to tell Daksh so.

'I was ashamed.' His brother spoke suddenly. 'And full of guilt. That's why I didn't talk to you that day. I couldn't.'

It was such an unexpected confession that Nikhil didn't know what to say. He simply sat, every muscle in his body taut and still, unable to move.

His brain conjured up an image of Isla, and somehow that seemed to soothe his soul.

'I should never have left you to deal with him alone,' his brother continued, every word measured and heavy, as though he found it the hardest thing to say, as though he'd spent years rehearsing it. 'I knew what he was capable of.

Most of the time he managed to keep it to just a beating, with a black eye or bruises that took weeks to heal. But there were a number of times I ended up in hospital because of him. Once with a broken leg, twice with a broken arm, twice with broken ribs.'

'Broken ribs. A knife wound. And once he sliced the bottom of my feet.'

Daksh cursed, a hollow, rasping sound loaded with hatred and suppressed fury. Somehow, it made Nikhil feel better.

'I thought he wouldn't touch you,' Daksh bit out. 'Or at least that was what I told myself. I thought that he targeted me because I looked more like our mother. I guess I wanted to believe that so that when I got out I could justify not going back. The one time I did, when he'd come out of rehab, you never mentioned anything. But I should have come back. I should have known he'd turn on you once I was gone.'

'He didn't at first,' Nikhil heard himself say. 'That first time you came back, he hadn't done anything. He went into rehab, and kept it going for a few months. I thought he had changed, but with hindsight I think he was just scared in case the authorities cottoned on. Not that they were any good back then.'

'I should have said something but...'

'You were embarrassed,' Nikhil finished when his brother trailed off. 'A grown-up kid getting beaten by his father. I know that feeling only too well.'

'You never should have had to. I was the older brother; I should have taken care of you.'

'Eighteen months older.' Nikhil shook his head. 'I don't think I'd have come back either, in your position. Though I've blamed you for it, all these years.'

It was odd how things could change in a heart-beat. Decades of censure and bitterness, gone in the space of half a conversation.

Because of Isla, a voice whispered. But Nikhil shut it down. She deserved better than him. She deserved a man who was good and true, who didn't have a black heart. At last Daksh had owned up to his mistakes, whilst he still hadn't faced up to his.

Maybe now was the time—there would be no other.

'I killed him, you know.' The confession scraped inside him, cutting and twisting as it left his body. And yet, even with the words out there, he felt something inside him begin to stir to life.

'No,' Daksh bit out instantly. Harshly. 'No, you didn't.'

'I had a knife.' For the first time in forever, Nikhil let his mind go back to that night, the silhouettes beginning to take better shape as the fog finally, finally began to lift. 'I stuck it in him.'

'No, you didn't.' Daksh recoiled, and Nikhil suddenly hated the horrified expression on his face.

It was extraordinary to find that after all these years he still sought his big brother's approval. He still felt lacking when Daksh looked at him with anything other than love. And still Nikhil forced himself to continue.

'I did. He was raging, and he had a knife. We wrestled and I managed to take it from him, I remember that. But then I felt suddenly angry, so angry, and he was still coming at me, and…then he wasn't.' Nikhil swallowed. 'I looked down, and there was blood, so much blood, and then his body was slumping on top of mine and I knew.'

'Christ, Nikhil…' His immaculate brother raked his hand through his hair, looking dazed. As if the two of them had just gone ten rounds.

'He was a monster, yes,' Nikhil ground out. 'But he didn't deserve to die. Not by his own son's hand.'

'You didn't kill him, Nik.' The unexpected nickname fired a salvo of memories at him, bombarding his head and bursting in his chest. 'Have you believed that all these years?'

'I remember it,' Nikhil managed harshly.

'You remember it wrong.'

Daksh sounded so certain, so angry, that Nikhil hesitated. It was as though he was standing right on the edge of some black, bottomless precipice—he wanted to back away; he just didn't know how to.

'You weren't there, Daksh.' He shook his head.

'But I read the police report.'

Snapping his head up, Nikhil could only stare at his brother.

'Not that I would care if you *had* killed him. He deserved it. But did you never wonder why, if you had killed him, you'd never been arrested?'

Nikhil felt as though his brain was swimming through treacle.

'I thought it was because I was fifteen, and there were no witnesses.'

'No, Nik, it's because you never did it. A neighbour heard the noise and they called the police. By the time they broke the door down, you were still in the position you'd been. Slumped on the floor with your back to the wall, and Dad on top of you.'

'But the knife was in my hand. It was in him.'

'The knife was there, in him, yes. But you

didn't go for him. He put that knife right through your shoulder, didn't he? Pinning you to the wall? Your blood was on the knife, and the wall—it all fitted.'

'Yes…' Nikhil heard the voice but it took a moment to realise it was his own.

He'd never told anyone any of this—except for Isla—there was no way Daksh could have known it unless he had, indeed, read the report.

'The blood mark from your shoulder travelled down the wall, where you'd slid. There was no break, which means your body never left the wall.'

'No break?'

'None,' Daksh confirmed. 'Which means that if you didn't move off the wall, you couldn't have lunged for him. He had to have been the one to come at you again. And you were in the process of collapsing to the floor, Nikhil, so the only possible explanation is that he came at you too hard, maybe he stumbled, but, either way, he impaled himself.'

'No…?' Nikhil choked out.

Could it really have been that simple? Had he been carrying around a guilt, all these years, which had never been his to bear?

'Yes, Nikhil.' Daksh gritted his teeth. 'The angle of your hand, the force, it just wasn't there.

You didn't do anything, little brother. I would say you were just at the wrong place at the wrong time.'

'No.' Nikhil shook his head again.

Was he really not the monster he'd believed himself to be? Had he sent Isla away from him, to protect her from him, for no good reason?

'I killed my father,' he repeated dully. 'I'm a monster.'

He watched, almost in slow motion, as Daksh threw himself up from his seat and came to crouch in front of him, his hand grabbing the back of Nikhil's head and pulling until they were forehead to forehead. The way they used to do as kids.

'You're no monster, little brother,' he bit out hoarsely. '*He* was the monster. Always him. And me, for leaving you there to suffer at his hands.'

'You were never a monster,' Nikhil managed, lifting his own hand to grab the back of his brother's head too. Like the biggest, most important of all the pacts they'd ever made. 'Though if you were I'd forgive you. I'd always forgive you.'

And despite the fact that he knew one conversation couldn't undo decades of self-loathing and recrimination, it somehow felt as though they'd made that first crucial step. The one that was always the hardest to make.

As if some healing process had begun—just as Isla had predicted. And it never would have happened without her. She'd already begun to change him. To help him take that step out of his past.

How had he failed to see that before? Or had he just been denying it to himself?

He was an idiot.

'I spent years thinking I had left it too long for us to ever stand a chance of healing the rift between us. I'm glad it wasn't too late.'

'It's going to take time.' The words were out before Nikhil had time to think about them. 'But it isn't too late after all.'

Was there such a thing as *too late*? he wondered suddenly.

What about Isla? Was it too late with her?

CHAPTER FIFTEEN

'WHAT ARE YOU doing here, Nikhil?'

Her heart was hammering so loudly, so wildly, inside her ribcage. But she couldn't allow him to see it. She *wouldn't*.

'I owe you an apology, Isla.'

Isla. Not Little Doc. She should feel triumphant.

She didn't. She just felt shaky. Edgy. Her eyes were drinking him in greedily, when she shouldn't have cared at all. It was galling the way she noticed the fit of his clothing, black jeans and a rock band tee, far more casual than the uniform he had practically lived in—unless they'd been naked in each other's beds, of course.

She swallowed hard and his eyes caught hers immediately. They darkened, and in that moment she hated herself for her weakness, and hated him for noticing.

Except that this thing humming and coursing through her wasn't *hate*, not even close. It took her all the way back to that beachside bar, when she'd sat with Leo and they'd argued good-naturedly about whether the honeymoon couple frolicking in the waves had really been in love.

Even now, she could hear her stepsister asking if that would ever be her, and she could hear herself scoffing, *No chance.*

But she didn't feel like scoffing any more.

It took everything Isla had to shake her head and get back to her paperwork.

As if he didn't matter to her.

'That isn't necessary,' she managed.

'On the contrary,' he gritted out. 'It's long overdue.'

'I don't care. I don't want to hear it.'

'I went to speak with Dax,' he shocked her by saying suddenly. 'Just as you told me that I should.'

Isla wasn't sure what hit her hardest, the fact that he'd been to see his brother, or the fact that he'd said it was because *she* had told him to do so. Was it foolish to believe that she really had that much influence on him?

As much as her head was screaming at her not to turn back to him, she couldn't pretend she didn't want to hear it any longer.

Swinging around, almost in slow motion, she perched her bottom on the edge of the desk. Her arms dropped straight down each side, surreptitiously clutching the edge of the wood. Gripping it white-knuckle-tight, until she feared her fingernails would be damaged beyond all recognition.

But what was that compared to the way he'd damaged her heart?

And whose fault was that? a little voice whispered snidely in her head. She thrust it aside roughly.

'All right. I'm listening.'

'I should have told you what the Captain had advised me. I should have mentioned that appearing to be in a stable relationship with someone like you—an officer, a ship's doctor—would have enhanced my chances of promotion.'

'Yes,' she managed. 'You should have. But you didn't. Because you wanted it to look convincing, you wanted to make sure everyone was fooled, and what better way to achieve that than by ensuring that even *I* was fooled?'

'Yes,' he ground out, and her heart stalled. It faltered.

And in that moment Isla realised there was a part of herself that had hoped he would say something different. Something more palatable.

She'd been used. Lesson learned. She sucked in a breath and tried to make herself stand. Her very soul felt as though it was splintering, tearing apart, and if she was going to shatter into pieces then the least she wanted was to do it in private. Where he couldn't see her.

But her legs felt like jelly and all she could do was grip the desk tighter.

'Well…' She had no idea how she managed to sound so crisp. So cool. 'Thank you for finally being honest, if nothing else.'

'That's what I initially told myself I was doing, anyway,' Nikhil continued, taking a step closer to her, making every inch of her skin prickle with awareness. 'Yet who else knows about us? If I had honestly wanted to do that, then what was the point in us being so discreet?'

'You were playing the game,' she choked out.

'Only there was no game, not really. What we had felt too precious, too private, too *significant* to feed to the rumour mill. So maybe I initially told myself that getting into a relationship with you would be excusable if I could pretend to myself that it was a strategic career move, but I'm not sure the truth is that simple.'

The roaring sound in her ears was almost deafening. She didn't want to believe him. She didn't want to *hope*.

And yet…hope poured through her.

Nikhil sounded as though he was rolling the words around his head before he spoke them.

Testing them out, seeing how they fitted. As though this wasn't easy for him. As though this was a truth with which even Nikhil himself was only just coming to terms.

'I don't have relationships with colleagues.'

'I'm know that.' She tried not to sound so bitter. Or hurt. 'You're too dedicated. Too career-driven to be distracted.'

'I never wanted to be in maritime,' Nikhil countered unexpectedly, and it wasn't so much an answer, Isla felt, as a tangent. 'In fact, it was the last thing I ever wanted to do. My father was a sailor; he worked in the boiler room, and I never wanted to do anything, *be* anything, remotely like him. For obvious reasons.'

No, she could understand that. Why would anyone want to follow in the footsteps of a violent, abusive drunkard who had caused so much pain? Mentally and physically.

'Then why join?' Isla asked, unable to help herself.

'Because there were scant other opportunities where I came from.' He shrugged. 'And so I decided that even if I had no other real option but to follow in his footsteps to join the profession, then at least I could make myself into the kind of man, the kind of sailor, that he'd never been. I could be the one thing he could never have even dreamed of—an officer.'

Which explained why he was dedicated, Isla supposed. Along with the way he had seemed to blame himself for how his father had died. Her mind raced. What had his brother said to him? Whatever it was, it must have been significant to bring Nikhil back here now.

Back to her.

'You never escaped him though, did you?' she asked quietly. 'You say you wanted to make yourself into an officer—something that your father could never have been—and yet you still let him haunt you all these years.'

'I did, but not because of him. More because of Dax.'

She wanted to speak, to answer, but she found she couldn't. Her mouth felt too dry, her tongue too thick. Even her body felt too tight in her own skin.

'I could say that I went to meet with him because of you, *pyar*. And perhaps I did. But I also went to meet with him because I needed to. I've needed to for probably twenty years, but I never had the courage before.'

'Before?' she croaked, as he nodded slowly and took a step closer to her.

'I didn't have it in me before you, Isla. But you

have changed everything. You've changed me. And I don't want to go back to the man I was before you came along.'

The kick in her chest was ferocious. And savage. And yet it was more breathtaking than brutal.

He *loved* her. He might not be able to say the word itself, yet the admission was there in everything he was describing. Still, she needed to hear more.

To be sure.

'What did he say? Your brother?'

'The day of that demon's funeral—when I saw the blame and loathing on Dax's face—my life changed. I thought I really was that monster that I saw whenever I looked in the mirror. But today I met with my brother...'

He tailed off, shaking his head as though he still couldn't believe it, and Isla couldn't hold herself back any more. She closed the remaining space between them, placing her hand on Nikhil's chest and feeling the pounding of his heart. It slammed into her palm, the beat fusing with the one drumming through her own body.

Almost as one.

'He didn't blame you, did he?' she asked, almost breathless.

'No.' Nikhil's eyes shone with a light she didn't

think she'd ever seen before. 'He blamed himself. He thought he should never have left me alone with that man.'

'He was little more than a kid himself,' Isla countered softly. 'Seventeen, I think you said.'

The corners of Nikhil's mouth pulled upwards as he reached out one hand to cup her cheek.

And, God help her, she couldn't bring herself to pull away.

'I know that, *pyar*. Do not fear, I do not blame him—at least, not any more. There have been enough recriminations and blame going around for too long. When the only one really to blame for it all has been long gone.'

'So, you and Dax have made your peace?' she asked hesitantly.

'We...are on our way to something like peace,' corrected Nikhil. 'Let us start with that, for now.'

Isla opened her mouth to answer, but the words didn't come. They were locked in some chaotic mess. As relieved as a part of her was for Nikhil, another part of her was still trying to work out how all that came together to bring him to her door.

'And this is your simple truth?' she managed after what felt like an eternity, lifting her own hand to cover his.

Though whether to cup his hand or to remove it, she couldn't quite be certain.

'No.' He shook his head, taking a final step to her and lifting his hand until he was cupping her jaw.

It was all she could do not to melt into it.

'No, the simple truth, *pyar,* is that I love you.'

The words walloped through her, leaving her winded. Any response was impossible; too many emotions were swooping and tumbling through her.

Nikhil loved her.

Just as she loved him. It was so obvious to her now.

'In fact,' he continued, as if oblivious, 'I think I've been falling in love with you ever since that first day on the quayside.'

Isla flushed instinctively. 'Maybe not that *first* moment,' she muttered awkwardly, but then Nikhil caught her upper arms, holding her tight and making her look at him.

'Yes. That first moment.' He nodded soberly. 'When you told me to *wind your neck in.* I think a part of me knew, right there, that you were the one for me.'

Isla tried to answer. She opened her mouth to speak, but nothing came out. She *loved* him. It should be terrifying, but Nikhil was taking all her fears and turning them on their head. And she liked it.

Maybe too much.

Because there were still so many other hurdles they hadn't even begun to overcome. How could she just pretend they didn't exist? However much she wished that to be the case.

'I want to be with you,' he told her. 'I want to share the rest of my life with you. Waking up to you. Going to bed with you. And everything in between.'

Her heart wanted to soar. She could feel it, pulling frantically at the tethers she'd used to ground it. To suppress it.

She didn't know how she found the strength to curl her fingers around his hand and pull it away from her face.

And then to drop the contact.

'I am pleased for you and your brother.' Her voice was more clipped than she would have preferred, but that couldn't be helped.

It was that or crumble completely.

'More pleased than you can imagine. But I'm confused at what you're saying. I have a posting as a doctor on a new ship, and you're getting your own ship to captain.'

His eyes gleamed but he didn't speak.

'So I fail to see how the two things are compatible,' she pressed on. 'Or is that the point? Now that you are secure in the knowledge that our lives are back on different courses, you realised that you felt safe enough to say the things you were too afraid to acknowledge before?'

'No. But I did realise something else.'

'What's that?' Her tongue spoke all by itself. And they both knew he had her where he wanted her. She despaired of herself.

'That was the moment I realised that I should walk away from you. And the moment I realised that I couldn't. And it had nothing to do with being secure in the knowledge that our lives were on different courses. I told you, it was to do with the fact that I am in love with you.'

And she wanted to argue. Or, more to the point, she didn't want to fall for words she'd been so desperate to hear. But she was finding it harder and harder to resist.

Then something else struck her.

'What do you mean, *our lives* were *on different courses?*'

He smiled. The most genuine, open smile she'd ever seen him give. And the tethers on her heart ripped and failed at that moment.

'I spoke to Head Office this morning.'

'If you changed my job again…'

'I never mentioned your job, Isla.' He silenced

her with a look. 'I discussed my own career path alone. And I suggested that I might prefer to run one more cruise as First Officer before I take up a post as captain. But this time I want to run it aboard the *Star of Hermione*.'

'That's my ship,' Isla gasped, her head spinning wildly, like a kid's paper windmill in a beach breeze.

She fought to cling onto reality. It wasn't right. It couldn't be. She had to be hearing things. Conjuring up the words that part of her so desperately wanted to hear.

'Yes, your ship,' he echoed, as though reading her doubts.

And allaying them one by one, as if he really did care. As if he really did *love* her.

Her whole world was exploding—going up like the most spectacular New Year's firework celebration. Almost too perfect to be true.

She shook her head, trying to think straight.

'You would turn down captaincy of a ship, and move from a flagship vessel like the *Cassiopeia*, just to be on the same ship as me? Meeting up in the shadows like we did for those two weeks?'

And God help her if she couldn't pretend to herself that they hadn't been two almost perfect weeks.

'You misunderstand.' Nikhil cut across her

thoughts. 'I don't want to hide in the shadows any more. I want this above board, if you'll excuse the pun, and I want us to be a proper couple.'

'A proper couple?' she echoed in disbelief.

'We would declare our relationship to Head Office and have them allocate us a cabin together. You are mine, just as I am yours. There will never be anybody else for me but you. And I no longer care who knows it.'

'You don't have to do that, Nikhil...'

'I love you, Isla,' he cut in. 'It's that simple. And maybe one day you'll be able to tell me that you love me too.'

'I already love you.' The words tripped off her tongue.

That easily.

'Isla...'

And this time it was her who cut him off.

'I love you, Nikhil,' she repeated, and wasn't it incredible how each time she said it something feverish, and glorious, filled her from the inside out?

'You are mine,' she echoed softly. 'And I am yours.'

Isla had no idea who moved first; she didn't particularly care. She only knew that one moment they were standing apart, where an entire continent might have divided them and it wouldn't have made her feel any more distant from him than she already felt—and the next she was back in his arms, her body moulded to his.

As if it had always been meant to be there.

'The more people who know it, the better, I think,' she murmured, moments before tilting her head up and pressing her lips to his.

'The world?' he muttered against her mouth.

'It's a start.'

The most magnificent start she could ever have imagined.

EPILOGUE

STANDING AT THE prow of the *Star of Hermione*, the sun setting behind her, Isla reflected that the past seven months with Nikhil, and two consecutive voyages as a proper couple, had possibly been the best of her life.

But now she was waiting, her heart once again pounding in her chest, as Nikhil had been summoned to the Captain's cabin. A part of her celebrated the fact that it could only mean he had already been offered a new captaincy, whilst another part of her was terrified.

She'd already been unofficially approached about joining the *Hestia*, the ship she'd been intended to join almost a year ago now, that first day back in Chile. But it was surely too much to hope that Nikhil had been offered captaincy.

Whichever ship they offered him, he couldn't turn it down a second time, she knew that, but it would mean the end of their perfect little bubble.

She turned as she heard the sound of his soft footfall across the deck.

'Which ship?' she asked without preamble, forcing herself to inject a note of excitement into her tone.

He eyed her speculatively, but there was no mistaking that hint of shock in his expression that could only mean it was better than either of them had anticipated for him.

As much as she was proud on his behalf, a little corner of her heart seemed to crumble a little. They had been so happy together on the *Hermione*. How was their relationship to survive such a move? Not that she didn't trust him. Unlike Brad, she had no fears that Nikhil would ever betray her; it simply wasn't who he was. But that distance just made things that much...duller.

Still, Isla was determined to betray none of those qualms as she forced herself to smile at him.

'Which ship, Nikhil?' she repeated.

'It is scarcely to be believed,' he managed, and there was an edge to his tone that was as unsettling as it was unfamiliar.

Her brain spun. 'Not the *Hestia*?'

'Not the *Hestia*,' he confirmed.

'Then which?'

'The *Cassiopeia*.'

Disbelief swirled around her and, despite the

fact that her heart still felt as though it was under arrest, she was incredibly proud of Nikhil.

Her Nikhil.

'That's amazing.' She threw her arms around his neck and embraced him as fiercely as she could. 'Really, I'm so pleased for you.'

'Well, there is something more.' He caught her face between his hands, holding her still so that he could talk to her. 'Dr Turner has been champing at the bit to get you back ever since you left.'

'Sorry?' She froze, scarcely believing it.

'The Captain asked me if I thought you'd be interested. I told him you probably wouldn't, but that I'd ask you just in case.'

'You said what?' she cried, disbelief flooding through her, moments before she realised he was teasing her.

'Nikhil, that isn't funny.'

'It is from where I am standing, *pyar.*'

The nausea began to lift. 'So that isn't what you really said?'

'Of course not.' He looked amused. 'I told him I would pass the message on and you would find him when you had an answer.'

'You didn't accept?' she cried, appalled.

Did Nikhil not want her to join him on the *Cassiopeia*?

'Of course I didn't accept, *pyar.* I have long

since learned my lesson regarding interfering in your career.'

'But you want me to join you?' She tried not to feel anxious, but it was impossible. Nikhil still had that odd edge about him, and it was disconcerting her more and more. 'Nikhil, what is it?'

He paused, and her stomach rolled.

'I was going to wait but...' He didn't quite shrug, but it was close.

'Nikhil?'

He swept his hand around and, whatever Isla had been expecting—or fearing—it certainly hadn't been to see a box in his hand. A small leather box with the finest gold filigree, that could surely only be one thing...

'Nikhil...' she echoed.

'I was going to give you this when we reached Hamburg tomorrow. But I don't think I can wait to hear your answer any longer.'

He opened the case, and Isla couldn't help gasping as a stunning pear-shaped ruby set in a cluster of shimmering diamonds winked up at her, so glorious that they seemed to reflect the very beauty of the sunrise itself.

'You saved my life, Dr Sinclair. I could never have imagined my life as full and as wonderful as it is without you in it,' he told her soberly. 'I love you more with each passing day, and I don't want to spend a single one of them without you in it. You chased away all of my nightmares, so marry me, *pyar*, and make the rest of my life a series of dreams instead?'

'You aren't the only one to have been saved when we met,' Isla choked out. 'My life would never have been so complete if I hadn't met you that day in Chile. I love you, Nikhil. Of course I'll marry you. I can't imagine my life without you.'

Slipping the ring on her finger, he finally kissed her—a kiss full of unspoken promises—and then he turned her around again. Her back nestled against his reassuringly solid chest and, his arms enveloping her, they stared towards the glorious sunrise on the horizon ahead.

It felt as if it wasn't just a new day. It was a whole new life. And it was going to be a glorious one.

Together.

* * * * *

LET'S TALK
Romance

For exclusive extracts, competitions
and special offers, find us online:

f facebook.com/millsandboon

◎ @millsandboonuk

🐦 @millsandboon

Or get in touch on 0844 844 1351*

For all the latest titles coming soon,
visit millsandboon.co.uk/nextmonth

*Calls cost 7p per minute plus your phone company's price per
minute access charge